Casper

Book I

El Cuento De Amor De Un Gangster

A Gangster Love Story

Akila Cruz
Ray Childress

Cotorra Books
c/o Casper – Book I
P.O. Box 37118
Oak Park, MI 48237
www.cotorrabooks.com

Front Cover Designed by:
Keith Saunders of Marion Designs – Stockbridge, GA
www.mariondesigns.com

Printed in the USA
First Edition – Book 1 of 10

Acknowledgments

First off... I'd like to 'Big Up' those that supported me and rode with me while I attempted to pump out this book series on this obsolete prison typewriter.

Thanks and love to my mother, Beverly.

My son, Rashaad: <shaadtall@yahoo.com>.

My sisters: Debbie, Erica and Terri.

My cousins: Gina Troup and Danika Childress-Jackson.

My Bro-In-Law: Brent Quarles.

And to My Peoples:

Dame Givner, Kevin Rucker, Dorian 'Nafis' Morefield, Wayne 'Way Loc' Allen, William 'Ricky' Boyd, Orande 'Man Loc' Shelton, Steve 'Irish' McLucky, Ilan Redman, 'G' Morefield, Leon 'Bit' Ford, Ricardo 'Reek' Montak, Candis 'CeDee' Thomas, Kina Davis, Rome 'Chrome' Soloman, Kalief 'Lief' Rethage, <olufemiyoung@gmail.com>, <shealynflowers@ymail.com>, Daniel 'Dunn' Castro, Fatima Baskin, Fernando 'Fiz' Gonzales, 'T' Coles, 'Vic' Victor, Ismael 'Izzy' Ortiz, Elia Pagan, Marcus 'Doe Boy' Suarez, Lester 'Lec' Pagan, Hector 'Hec' Avilez, The God: I-Real Unique, Bolibar 'Bolas' Barrios, 'P.R.', Maldonado-Cruz, Ruben 'Brue' Sanchez, 'Papo' Ramos, Carlos 'Los' Garcia, 'Lil Rooster' Mickens, Derrick 'Big Damu' Crooms, Norman 'Slim' Williams, Garriston 'C-Crazy' Shyne, Nathaniel 'Reds' Clark, 'Mal' Childs, Troy 'Red-Rum' Brown.

And now last, but certainly not least, Mil...That friend that came through for me with that motivation to complete this 10 book series.

Prologue

On a pleasant day back in 1984 a wiry built, dark Chicano by the name of Ricardo Alvarez drove his freshly painted grey-on-grey El Camino low-rider down Southern California's 91 Freeway, bobbing his head to the smooth sounds of Santana's "Oye Como Va' – his young, yet calculated mind focused on the changes he was preparing to make to his life.

Ricardo chuckled at his own paranoia after reaching to check his new stash spot for the second time in the last half hour; he'd just had the car's interior redone down in Mexico, and he wasn't all that secure with the new hiding spot for his black 380 handgun. "Kick back, Ho'lllmes." He said aloud to admonish himself before fingering his neatly trimmed goatee.

Though not an overly cocky young man, Ricardo did carry himself with a cool quiet Confidence. And that along with his rugged good looks seemed to draw beautiful young women to him in droves, something he had no problem accommodating—up until a few months ago when he met Anna.

A fresh, cocky grin creased his lips at the thought of Anna. She was the reason he was driving back from Riverside after pulling a couple of all-nighter's at one of his set's dope-houses where profit margins were nearly double of what he'd make back in L.A., on his gang's 18th Street turf. Ricardo needed to get his money right in a hurry to make a pre-planned, 30 thousand dollar heroin purchase in preparation for his cross-county move with Anna and her daughter.

Known throughout the barrios as El Fantasma (The Ghost), a placa (nickname) that struck a touch of apprehension in the most hardened of his set's enemies; Ricardo, barley into his 20's, was already being mentioned by elite gangbangers walking the yards of prisons like Chino, Lompoc, Pelican Bay and San Quentin—but 'The Life' as they called it, was no longer what he aspired to. His chance meeting and subsequent burgeoning relationship with the shapely black girl by the name of Anna had changed all of that.

Anna had caught Ricardo's attention in the supermarket parking lot that sunny afternoon when she slowly turned and unknowingly gave him a shot of her amazing side profile. 'Cho (Whoa)!' He had gasped, tapping his closed fist to his lips. Her goddess-like looks made him think of nothing but taking his pleasure.. Having grown up with black homeboys and homegirls within his 18th Street set, Ricardo was not adverse to a darker shade of chica—but once he approached her in that parking lot and began to rope her in for the kill, something foreign to him occurred. He fell

2

hard for her creamy chocolate skin, along with her sassy East Coast attitude.

The young couple became inseparable almost immediately; spending every waking moment together. Then, one day while riding back from a day at Venice Beach, Anna asked him to take a leap of faith.

"Why don't chu move back East with me?" She asked the question as if it were no more than a request for a stick of gum.

The choice to move out to the Northeastern part of the country was easy for Ricardo, due to a gangbanger's short shelf life in South Central. He knew if he did not make a 'life change' right now, his path would lead to one of two places—an early grave or an extended stay in a prison cell. And having already tasted the waters of California's Youth Authority system known as Y.A.; he wasn't all that eager to start spending time behind penitentiary walls. "I don't need dat shit!" Ricardo grumbled as he hit the turn signal to take the Compton exit off of the 91 Freeway.

Before heading home, Ricardo had decided to take one last shot at softening his mother's resolve toward Anna and his relationship.

Unbeknownst to Ricardo as he dwelt on his Madre's (mother's) hatred for his girl, two beautiful Bandidas on the far side of the boulevard's divide scoped-out him and his shiny Dayton rims. Both young women rolling in the customized van wore the big hairstyles of the Cholas (Gangster Girls), with dark eyeliner outlining their eyes and their dark-colored lipstick… 'Si solo las miradas mataran (If looks could kill).'

3

The Cholas continued to eye what they could see of the dark, nicely built Chicano in his crisp, white wifebeater—catching a tingle or two as the muscles in his shoulders and biceps rippled with the effort of whipping the grey 'low-low' sitting on deep dish chrome Dayton wires, right, onto Greenleaf street.

"Siiii (Yeh-hesss)!" Rosa hissed sexily as she leaned forward in the van's passenger seat, "Homegirl, I'd fuck his brains out…"

Ricardo hit the hydraulic switch and raised the El Camino to its full height to deal with the speed bumps within the Compton neighborhood's inner blocks.

Rosa had begun to touch-up her plum-colored lipstick while telling her homegirl in rapid fire Espanol, to hurry up and bust a U-turn so they could catch the dark muchacho… Even though both young women had the look of petite angels, either of them could kill in cold blood at the drop of a dime.

"Heeee…" Rosa whined in almost a hum as that familiar feel of a flip-flopping sensation arose inside her belly. She could envision herself having sex with the guy driving the El Camino while her homegirl watched, and waited to join in—prior to them murdering him and being on their way with his ride.

Throughout Southern California the Dayton rims were referred to as 'Killer Daytons' for a good reason—young men were dying left and right over the shiny, spoke rims; and these particular Bandidas had a penchant for the caper. They loved fulfilling their sick sexual inclination to rob and murder, with the added intoxication of wild sex.

The beautiful Cholas had once lured a high volume dealer of sherm (PCP), to a seedy motel at the end of the 91 Freeway known as the 'Dare You Inn', where while in the midst of a wild, steamy, drug induced three-way sex session, they began to stab him repeatedly—prior to covering themselves with the dead man's bright red blood while continuing to use the man's rather sizable, still erect penis to pleasure each other for some time.

But luckily for Ricardo, on this day the Cholas were on their way to a big cookout over in the city of Carson, and the driver of the van, Camila, did not want to risk getting blood on her long, white traditional tunic gown.

* * *

As Ricardo rode down Greenleaf, he nearly made a right turn onto Oleander Street, which would have taken him into the Farm Dog neighborhood where his novia (sweetheart) had stayed with her familia before going back East last week.

"Huhhh!" Ricardo released a deep sigh. It had only been a week, but he already missed Anna like crazy. He longed to look into her dark-brown, doe-shaped eyes. She was almost too good to be true for him. He could sit and talk with her for hours about anything from the streets to his artwork— nothing with her seemed to ever bore him.

But as with most hot-blooded young males, his mind drifted toward her lush curves and their fervent love making; which was unlike anything he'd ever experienced. Anna had this way of chewing at her bottom lip as her agile hips rolled and swiveled

5

with the lusty movements of her riding him while his hands roamed from her shapely, plump rear end to fondle her softly shuddering mounds of juicy breast flesh. "Uhmmm..." he was reminded of the way her breath would come in a ragged little tell-tale rush, almost a hum just as she reached her apex.

Ricardo had his share of amorous, salacious young chicas, so he never felt like Anna and his relationship had anything to do with him being "pussy whipped". But MAN did she have the ability to take him places! And not just with her sex; sometimes he would find himself simply watching the way her eyes played with him...intrigued him.

"Neva thought I'd miss all that attitude, either." He mused as he rode over the train tracks and turned into the Spook Town neighborhood to have a word with his uncle Lalo...

"What dat Spook Town look like, Ese'eeee!" A tall skinny Mexican wolfed at Ricardo as he pulled up in front of his grandmother's house.

"Sup, Vato Loco (Crazy Nigga)!" Ricardo barked back at his uncle.

Lalo leaned back in his gangster pose and adjusted the wide-folded brown bandana down low on his brow. He then began to groove to the lyrics of the smooth chorus flowing from the speakers inside his nephews El Camino.

"Oh, Lord. Please don't let me be misunderstood." Twisting his fingers appropriately, Lalo threw-up his Spook Town set's gang sign. He wore his blue Dickie's suit, with the pants cut into below the knees shorts, displaying the look of a true Compton gangbanger as the low-rider classic put him in a mood to smoke some water (PCP) and hunt enemies.

Ricardo stepped away from the car so his uncle could check out the grey, crushed velvet interior. "Tu like?"

Lalo nodded smoothly, slicking back the top of his neatly cut jet black hair—loving the silver flakes within the highly glossed paint job. "Ho'lllmes..." He allowed the L's to roll from his tongue in praise. "18th Street rakin'it in, ey?"

Smoothing back his own, equally, dark slick head of hair, Ricardo grinned from ear-to-ear. "Loco, Ese..." He nodded confidently, pulled up his oversized tan khakis and adjusted the extra length of belt to hand just right. "We doin' our t'ing."

"Riiiiight, riiight." He strolled around the low-low, admiring its sleek style. "I see..."

"Where's mi abuelita (grandma)?" Ricardo asked.

"Ayer (Yesterday), her and jour madre (moms) went down to San Diego to visit de' familia."

"Pshhhhh!" Ricardo puffed out a hard gust of breath. He needed to speak with his abuelita to try to get her to reason with his madre.

Momma Alvarez had a serious problem with her son getting into a relationship with a girl she liked to refer to as 'Puta Mayate (Nigger Bitch), after Ricardo brought her into their home to view the mural he'd painted.

"Lalo, I need her to put in a good word for me."

"Decirunas palabras en favor de (To put in a good word)?" Lalo folded his arms and leaned back into a gangster stance, eyeing his young nephew suspiciously… "Chu tryin' to get her to smooth shit out so jhu can shack'up with de'lindo (lovely) chocolate chica chu been hanging out with. Huh, Vato?"

Ricardo frowned and looked away to keep his uncle from seeing the smile that threatened to break across his lips. "Stall me out, Lalo."

He slammed an open palm onto his shoulder. "She got jour nose wide open, don't she?"

Ricardo's dark eyes went downward, to stare at the tips of his black Chuck Taylor's.

"You sure you can handle all of that mujer (woman)?" Lalo continued to clown with him. "She is workin' with some serious curves on that pequena (little) body of hers."

"O'ye (Hey)!" He cut his uncle off.

"Yo!" Lalo danced away as his nephew closed the distance. "I'm de mulfucka that taught chu how to slang them dogs."

Ricardo did not budge when Lalo fired a few quick jabs near his nose. "I'm not fuckin' around. Esta mierda es muy serio (This is some serious shit)."

Sensing the seriousness of the situation, Lalo turned it down a notch.. "I can tell jhu right now. Mi sis is not about to change her mind on this one, she's old school." He looked down at his own forearm to stress the point. "Ves como el piel de nosostro es oscuro (See how dark our skin is) Carnal (Brother)? Pure Mexicano!"

Ricardo's eyes dropped a second time, although he wasn't ready to give up. "Yo nececito ayuda (I need some help)."

Just as Ricardo's uncle began to speak, an unmarked narc car slow-rolled around the corner.

8

Ricardo watched the two plain clothed Compton undercover cops eyeing him as they pulled to a stop. For a brief second, he thought about taking off. *Nah, fuck'it,* he thought. *I'm limpio (clean)!*

The white cop with the blonde hair exited first, from the driver's side—followed by this big black partner.

"It's Blondie and Bookman." Lalo said out of the side of his mouth as he stepped to the curb to greet the two officers, who were about as fair as they came when dealing with cops working the ghetto. "Yo! Whass'up wit'chu fools rollin' up in my hood like y'all fixin' to blast?"

As was his easy going nature, Blondie laughed him off. "Ho'lllmes... All I'm doin' is making sure the streets are safe for good law abiding citizens like yourself."

Lalo flashed him a look like, *Who me?*

Meanwhile Bookman silently walked around the El Camino and checked out the car, along with its owner.

"This your ride?" Blondie asked from over by the gate where he stood with Lalo.

Ricardo nodded as he continued to lean against the car's trunk. *These cops ain't nothin' like the ones in L.A., 'cause we'd be lying on the dirty ground by now.*

Blondie knew Lalo was clean before he exited the car. But the unfamiliar was a different story. *Yeah, he's a lot stronger than he looks.* He thought, as he sized-up Ricardo, *One of those wiry kids... and those eyes.* He could always tell who the real stone-cold killers were by their eyes. "Lalo, I'mma have to run your nephew's name."

"C'mon wit' all that, man. You makin' me look bad out here." Lalo's attempt to cop a plea wasn't going so well.

The blonde cop shrugged and tugged at his mustache, "Look, if he's as clean as you say, I owe you one."

Ricardo went on leaning against the trunk as his name was read to the operator over the car radio—confident as can be his thoughts drifted to Anna and the tight, two-toned designer jeans she had on the last time he saw her. *Man, and that mean walk...*

"ALVAREZ!"

The cop's sharp tone made him flinch.

"Pon tus manos arriba del cofre (Place your hands atop the trunk)!" Blondie ordered.

"Fuck!" Ricardo sneered as the cops drew their guns.

* * *

A year and several months later, Ricardo found himself on a foul smelling prison bus, headed up North. He'd been wrongly implicated in an armed robbery that was committed by some El Salvadorans from the Pico and Union section of his 18th Street gang. And like a true G, he kept his mouth shut and took his cut. Ricardo looked at it like, FUCK IT! *Mi vida loca.* He knew he'd done a lot of things that could have got him anywhere from a life sentence, to the gas chamber.

As Ricardo stared out through the caged bus windows at the peaks of the snow capped mountains rolling along in the distance beneath the blue sky, he thought about Anna. Though it felt good to have stepped up like a man to take the prison bid on the chin, he regretted what became of Anna and his relationship after he was unable to get in contact with her during his stay in the L.A. county jail.

He knew of Anna's issues with abandonment, which led to him reminiscing over the first time they made love.. Ricardo had become unsettled by what seemed to him to be exaggerated tears afterward, until he learned that she had not been with another man since the murder of her daughter's father. Then, he smiled inwardly at the thought of a conversation that occurred later on in their relationship:

While lying in bed one evening, recuperating, Anna playfully bit into Ricardo's chest. "O'ye! Por que lo hizo (Hey! Why you do that)?" He asked as his hand slid down her back to palm a warm, bouncy ass cheek.

Anna released a coy, girlish giggle. "Yo no se (I don't know)."

"Ahaaa! I see jhu're learning mi language."

"I amm.. Amongst otha' things." She declared sweetly while twisting her full lips.

Ricardo felt himself begin to thicken, just by looking into her eyes. "Uh-Uhmm…" he cleared his throat. "Chu know I'll probably be de' first Mexican they ever seen out there."

"So what." Anna said with some attitude, before rubbing her soft cheek in a cat-like fashion to his strong chest. "Don't worry. I'm sure I'm more than capable of keepin' you warm on those cold Northeastern nights."

"What about de' days?" He asked with a chuckle as he began to knead the firm, pulpy flesh of her bottom.

11

She purred agreeably, "I'll take care of those too."

Ricardo's jaw clenched the moment the smell of a man releasing gas reached his nose, destroying the pleasantries of his daydream.. He'd been through his fair share of disputes in the county jail over the past few months, but the thoughts of Anna really struck a nerve. For one, he could not talk to her. For two, he'd learned via Lalo, that Anna had reached out to his familia with news that she'd given birth to his hijo (son).

* * *

An ongoing feud between the Surenos (Southern California Chicanos) and Nortenos (Northern California Chicanos) was in full escalation mode upon Ricardo's arrival at the prison, which dropped him right smack in the middle of a bloody war that had raged for years within California's prisons. And to make matters worse for Ricardo, the prisoner working the processing desk mistakenly placed Ricardo on the fresh meat block where he would be vigorously recruited, instead of putting him with his "So Cal" faction.

The instant Ricardo stepped into his new cell and laid his bed-roll down on his bunk, a tall burly Norteno O.G. came to his doorway. The man was so massive that his body blocked out most of the light. "Qu-Que pasa (What's up)?" Ricardo stammered out as his eyes searched for a light switch.

The huge man smelled fear, and he loved it. "Where jeu from, Vato?" He said in a thick No-Cal accent.

With the man's blue prison shirt unbuttoned, Ricardo was able to take in the tattoos covering his torso. Subsequently, his bottom lip turned up into a frown.

The big man made his first mistake when he underestimated Ricardo (The Ghost). Then he compounded that mistake by not pulling his knife fast enough.

The Ghost (El Fantasma) rushed straight into the bigger man's body with an eye-blinding quickness. But the big man briskly recovered and used his superior size to push El Fantasma further back into the small grey cell.

Fantasma uttered a growl as he grasped the knife hand of the man to prevent him from pulling the steel shank from his waist band. "Hurrgg!" he grunted from a head butt that split the bridge of his nose. Ricardo gritted his teeth and shook off the dizziness. *I am in a fight for mi vida.* He thought, as he began to rapidly blink his eye to clear the blood blurring his vision.

Grunts and growls bounced off of the tiny cell's walls as Fantasma and the big man tussled and fought for position.

"Yo puede sentir tu (I can feel you), weakeningggg." The man husked down into Fantasma's face, before bull-rushing him back into the sink and nearly breaking him in two.

Ricardo could not halt the slight whimpering-like sound that escaped his lips as a jolt of nauseating pain ripped through his body. The smell of the man's putrid breath started to suffocate him, wilt him. But he was still far from giving up as the bigger man had begun to think.

Then, by the luck of the draw, the big man slammed his own knife down into his thigh while trying to knee Ricardo.

The man's crazy eyes turned even wilder, intensifying as he peered down into the face of his smaller adversary. "Yo te voy a matar despacio, suei (I'm going to kill you, slow)." He growled thru his clenched, tobacco stained teeth.

Fantasma fired his knee up into the big man's groin, but the attempt was easily block.

"Ahaaa!" He smiled confidently, truly impressed with himself. "Yo te quiero vivo para que seas testigo que yo te rompi el madurez (I want you alive so you can witness me taking your manhood)."

Even with the perilous situation he already found himself in, that statement shook Fantasma to his core. He had to concentrate to slow his breathing. He needed to use all of his smarts to survive, *There is no way I can match this fool, strength-for-strength, in such close quarters.*

Fantasma planted his back foot hard, to keep from being forced backwards into the narrow space between the steel bunk and the toilet. He knew if he allowed himself to be shoved into that space, he would never leave the cell alive.

"Yo puede sentir tu, weakeningggg." The man continued to taunt. He became more and more overconfident due to his many years of strenuous weight training in the weight-pits throughout California's prison system. To him, Ricardo was of no account—he had taken apart several men superior in size and strength to the young scrapper.

Fantasma allowed the Norteno O.G. to believe he'd gained the upper hand, by letting go of the wrist of his knife-hand, which he'd been holding onto for dear life. He then fired a flat palm up thru the gap between the man's thick forearms, just as the man's fingers started to tighten around his neck.

CAR-RRRAAAAACK! The sickening wet sound echoed off of the wall as Fantasma's palm smashed flesh and nose cartilage. He moved in a continuous motion as if his moves were planned and outlined. He slung the disoriented man around by the collar of his shirt; propelling the bulky weight where he wanted it to go. Fantasma slammed him down over the toilet bowl, cracking his back over the porcelain seat. He followed that up by ripping the long, crudely made shank from his attacker's thigh and jamming it deeply into his barreled chest, forcing it through the cavity to puncture his heart.

"Farmeros!" Fantasma barked breathlessly as he stood over what was once a major shot-caller of the No-Cal army.. Even with the adrenaline still pursing through his veins, Ricardo was able to understand his urgent predicament. *I gotta find a way out of this.*

Ricardo knelt to gather his breath once he'd stuffed the body underneath his bunk and covered it with a blanket and some sheets.

Within minutes the cell block tier filled with the noise of prisoners filing out of their cells for chow-line. Fantasma scanned the faces swiftly before being blessed to come across a face he knew from East L.A. "Que pasa?"

Following a short greeting, Fantasma got straight to the point. "Quien es que corre este block para So-Cal (Who runs this block for So-Cal)?"

Fantasma sensed some reluctance within his solidly built friend. "Yo quiero conocera esta wuei."

The two young men stood eye-to-eye for a long pause after Fantasma's question. The young man from East L.A. wasn't all that eager to get involved in anything dealing with either of the warring sides. He had less than a year to do on his sentence and hoped to make it back to Boyle Heights in one piece. But due to his knowledge of Fantasma and his barrios's vicious reputation, he decided that it would probably be wiser to help him out.

Following chow, Fantasma's East L.A. amigo took him to meet with a Sureno out in the yard. Initially, the man refused to even speak to him until a very desperate Fantasma relayed to him a portion of what had gone down inside his cell. The man then told them to hold tight near the bleachers while he hustled off, prior to returning a short time later to usher Fantasma over to meet El Jefe (The Boss) face-to-face.

When Fantasma approached him on the far side of the prison yard's field house, the tall, slimly built grizzled vet stood there stoically, leaning his weight over on the wooden can he clutched within his strong weathered fist. El Jefe had been through so many prison wars over the years that he'd lost track: the Mayates, the Nortenos, the Aryans, it seemed to never end. He listened now as the jovencito (youngster) told him of a confrontation with El Animal, a dangerous Norteno enforcer. "Palabra, el estara aqui por ti (My word, he will come looking for you)." The old man advised Fantasma.

Fantasma raised his chin and pushed out his chest. "Yo lo mate en mi celda (I killed him inside my cell)."

The old man's graying eyebrows came together, "Where jhu get a pedaso (shank)?" a chuckle slipped free as he asked.

"I used his." This reply made El Jefe laugh in a bit of nervous disbelief. "Palabra!" Fantasma continued, as he brandished a cocky grin.

The confidence in which the jovencito spoke the word ceased the man's laughter. El Jefe could not hope to contain the grin that emerged on his usually stern face—a major blow had been struck to Nuestra Familia. *So this is de' young Ghost*, his head nodded in a show of approval.

Ricardo (Fantasma) lit up like a Christmas tree.

The old man reached out and placed his hand on Fantasma's shoulder, "I heard about'chu, por medio de chismes (through the grapevine)."

"Si?"

"Si." El Jefe's eyes continuously scanned their immediate area, "Yo te conosco su gentes (I know your folks).

That statement knocked Fantasma for a loop, "Que (Huh)?"

He went on to tell Fantasma that he used to run the streets with his dad, back when he was his age. "C'mon, I'll tell jhu all about it." El Jefe strode ahead, out onto the big yard's track to walk a few laps.

Fantasma observed the way that the oldtimer's homeboys drifted back to take up the rear, just as something came to him. "Uh, Senor, his body is still in mi cell."

The old man appeared to smirk as if the revelation hadn't bothered him in the least, "Tenemo que hace algo con esta cuelpo (We'll have to do something with that body)."

* * *

El Animal's body was discovered down in the prison laundry that very night, stuffed inside of a laundry cart full of dirty kitchen worker uniforms.

Over the next few days an all-out war exploded between the Surenos and Nortenos, claiming the life of the revered El Jefe, along with the lives of several other valuable members on both sides. The prison had become even more of a dangerous warzone as deadly attacks erupted around the clock— until the one referred to as the Ghost (El Fantasma), went extra "Cucui".

Like the shadowy ghostly figure he'd become, Fantasma snuck onto the Nortenos cell block and laid in wait under the bunk of Nuestra Familia's chief shot-caller. Then at just the right moment when the man lay down for his afternoon siesta, Fantasma reached up and grabbed a handful of the man's hair as he simultaneously drove a long, straightened ice pick through the thin mattress, directly into the base of his skull – efficiently severing the brain from the spinal cord stem.

Following the daring murder that would rock the other side to its core, Fantasma escaped without his presence ever truly being detected; which added to the Ghost's legend that would go on to reach epic status on the streets of California and throughout prisons stretching as far as the Mississippi River.

Chapter 1

East Coast - Winter of 2004

Fly, a 44 year old major hustler, eased his low-key Maxima sedan into a parking spot on the city's rough and tumble West side. Then he watched as his new flavor of the month, Stacy, stepped her curvaceous self from the car.

Stacy, playing her part, moved with just enough twerk in her hips to allow Fly a glimpse of her prominent booty. When, "Fuck!" a mean gust of wind hit her. She quickened her step around the car, as her wool, knee-length Chanel skirt did next to nothing to keep her warm.

The tipsy couple made their way up to the doorway of her row house, where Fly began to grind against her ass while she prolonged the search for her door keys.

"Hmmm." Stacy purred like a kitten in the instant Fly's hand slipped inside of her winter trench coat to palm one of her voluminous breasts. "Them Blue Dolphins kickin' in, huh?"

Stacy had persuaded her potential "sugar daddy" to pop an E-pill, along with Viagra before they left the club. And even though the young woman was 5 months pregnant, she dropped a double stack (2 ecstasy) herself. Stacy pretty much had no regard for her unborn child, herself, or her drug dealing, young thug of a baby-daddy, who just happened to control the blocks around her row house..

"Al'ight, ya spot is real nice." Fly smiled as Stacy headed up the stairs.

"Thank you!" She yelled down, prior to yelling for him to make himself comfortable. "Go ahead and put some music on, too."

Once in her bedroom, Stacy threw on a pink babydoll and went to check herself out in the mirror. "Uhm-hmm..." she turned side-to-side, "I'mma give that nigga the best pussy he eva' had."

Stacy had been hooking up with Fly, off and on for close to a month now. They would usually end up at a hotel or one of his "duck off" cribs, but tonight she was going for the takeover. It was time to go for what she had planned since that chilly afternoon when she ran into him at a downtown jewelry store. The memory was still fresh. She'd given him some sass and 22 year old attitude while knowing exactly who and what he was—a filthy rich O.G., who had a thing for fine, chocolate pregnant bitches..

Stacy came down the carpeted stairs in nothing but a pair of high-heeled Prada sandals and the sheer babydoll. She offered Fly a few twists and turns, then watched from under hooded eyes as he leaned back on the sofa to undo the iced-out buckle of his gator skinned belt. "Uh-uhnnn, Dad'ddyyy! Let me handle dat." She knelt in front of him..

"Hurgh…" Fly gasped and watched Stacy lick and slobber her way up and down his stiff pole before encircling its swollen heat with her thick lips.

"Umm-umph!" She moaned and continued to bob her head in a lustful manner while sucking down his first nutt of the evening. Undeterred by the quick eruption, she went to work with her pierced tongue, using a practiced professionalism. Stacy teased the slit in the mushroomed-shaped head with the tip of her tongue, prior to taking him deep down her throat. *I wish I had this nigga's baby in my belly, instead of young'ass Court's,* she pondered analytically as she inhaled and exhaled through her nose to provide the unbridled pleasures of her gullet.

Court was young and immature enough for Stacy to easily manipulate him with her advanced sex game. She would regularly perform tricks on her 19 year old lover that blew his mind—had him buying her furniture, jewelry, clothes, and even making the payments on her brand new Benz coupe. And although she did use him for his money; if Stacy were to be honest with herself, she'd admit that the young thug held a prominent place in her heart.

* * *

Meanwhile the young thug known on the Westside by the nickname Court, stood in the hallway of one of the Trackstone project highrises, listening to his young runner tell him that his B.M. was spotted in her doorway, hugged-up.

"Cuz," the youngster shook his head sympathetically, "Old dude was grindin' all up on her ass."

"Good look, lil homie." Court said, sending the young boy on his way as he began to contemplate how to go about handling the situation.

"What'chu wanna do?" Court's man Rabbit, anxiously barked.

His dull, dark eyes went to Rabbit, a childhood friend he knew secretly worshipped him. "You got'cha toast?"

Rabbit raised his jacket to show the 9mm handgun, "Always, Loc. You know how I rock."

"Let's do this then." Court said, leading the way out into the cold winter night…

Back at Stacy's house, the sounds of skin smacking into skin rose above the smooth love-making music as she willingly gave it up to Fly in the reverse-cowgirl position. "Ooooh shit!" She panted, digging her widely spread heels into the carpet to get better leverage to place her palms on her knees while she wildly bounced her ass in his lap. "Oooh-oooolll! Do-it! Do-itttt!" She cried.

"Uhh! Umph-uhm!" Fly grunted and gasped, totally unaware that Stacy was watching him from over her shoulder as he watched his cream-coated shaft slip in-and-out from in between her splayed cakes.

There was nothing but pure lust in her eyes as her tight, wet walls gripped and grabbed at Fly's slammer on the outstroke. "Oooh! Oh God!" Stacy suddenly eked out, "I'm-I'mma cum again!"

Due to the enhanced sensitivity from the ecstasy and Viagra pills, Fly's eyes cinched shut with the brisk approachment of his explosion…

After the two of their heart rates decreased and their breathing leisurely decelerated, Stacy's upward progress assisted her lover's nature to ease out of her. When she slowly turned around to face him, she gazed in his eyes before gradually dragging her tongue up the side of his cheek. "You thirsty, Daddy?" She whispered in his ear.

In the meantime, Court and Rabbit were creep'n outside of Stacy's crib. "Shut da FUCK up!" Court growled menacingly, as Rabbit asked another idiotic question. He slowly slid his key into the lock. *All I done did for this BITCH and she gon' play me for a lame,* he mused to himself. *She got some old fool puttin' dents in my baby's head? She knows how I get down.*

Court quietly opened the door and eased inside with Rabbit on his heels, guns drawn. The young men could hear the sounds of the slow jam crooner, Ginuwine, playing at a relatively low level as the back of a man's head lulled at the top of the new sofa.

They caught him slippin'.

"Nigga!" Court gritted through his teeth. "Don't move a fuckin' muscle."

This Bitch set me up! Was the first thought to shoot through Fly's head.

"Where's Stacy?" Court asked as he made his way around the sofa he'd bought.

"Yo!" Rabbit squealed with a hand over his mouth. "Old-head got a wet boner."

Court turned to his homie with a look that read, *if you say one more word.* And with a look like that, coming from the one who appeared to be top dog, Fly knew there was no set-up in play. *What the fuck have I gotten myself into,* he thought.

Stacy heard a familiar voice from the kitchen and stupidly stepped into the room. "Oh shit!"

Court looked up to see none other than his B.M. standing there butt-naked, looking super-thick with a light sheen of sweat causing her pregnancy swelled knockers to shine like polished globes. His eyes dropped lower to take in the slight bump of her belly, then lower to where the insides of her brown thighs shimmered with what looked to be splashed cooking oil.

"Court!" Stacy shrieked as she dropped both bottles of water and cupped her hands over her mouth. "Cour-."

"You is a scandalous BITCH!" Court snarled as he spoke to her with an utter disgust evident in his tone.

Stacy screeched and made a run for the backdoor—slipping and sliding in her sandals, only to be caught from behind by Rabbit.

"Where you goin'?" Rabbit husked against her ear as he pinned her naked body to the kitchen counter from the rear, out of the sight of Court. "Huh?"

Stacy had always known about Rabbit's crush on her and she would tease and taunt him at every turn.

"The dirty Lil' Flunky. Ain't that what'chu used to call me to my face? Whass'up?" His fingers dug painfully into her right breast. "Who dir-"

"Rab!" Court yelled from the front room.

"Go!" Rabbit pushed her into the living room.

Court watched Stacy get shoved to the floor. "Who's this old'ass nigga?" He jutted his chin at Fly.

Stacy's eyes seemed to light up as a cocky smirk came to her lips. "Oh. I know you heard of Fly? From Wilson Works..."

Court swallowed the huge lump that tried to rise up his throat—and then he gathered himself. "Uh, look O.G.," he pinched at the bridge of his nose. "I respect who you is an all dat. But'chu ran up in the wrong shot of ass on this trip."

Fly could do nothing but listen as Rabbit was ordered to search the pockets of his pants lying over the back of a chair.

"Rab, grab dat Mont Blanc wrist watch off him too. Oh! And check that butta' leather over dere. You know an O.G. like him ain't rollin' way over here wit'out no cannon (gun)."

By this time, Stacy had calmed down some and began to calculate, *I know dis nigga ain't gon' buss my head. Shit, I'm carrying his seed.*

Court looked at Stacy as if he'd read her mind. "Rab. Tie up both of 'em."

"Yo! HOL'LLLD UP! Wha-wait a minute." Stacy attempted to protest before she was turned face-down, while her hands were tied behind her back...

Court and Rabbit ransacked the house for the next half an hour—pocketing valuable jewelry along with the money from a small safe he kept inside of Stacy's closet.

Stacy craned her neck to look up at Court when he came back into the living room and stood over her. "Boo, we can work this out."

Court's eyes slowly glanced down to take in the sight of her prone on her face; hog-tied, hands behind her back—almost kneeling in some sort of S&M position. "Ah! Haa! Haaa!" He grunted with each kick and stomp that landed to Stacy's back and head. "Is thisss what-chu-want? HUH! Huh?"

"Nooo! No! I'm sorry! Da' BABY!" She screamed out.

"Bitch! It prob'ly-aint-even-MINE!" Court punctuated each word with his foot kicking her in her bare ass. He then stood there huffing for air between chuckles of breathless laughter, as she curled herself into a ball. "Oh, that's right. You a tough bitch, ain't chu?"

Through eyes filled with tears, Stacy peered up at something she never seen. Court had flipped the switch and turned into the monster she'd heard he was in the street.

Court turned and glared at Rabbit going through one of the bags by the front door. "Rab, c'mere."

"Whass'up, Cuz?" The short, brown-skinned young man pulled at the waist of his extra baggy jeans and walked across the room.

"You wanna fuck dis hoe?" Court stared down at Stacy as the question left his lips.

Rabbit's eyes dropped to his unlaced Timberland boots. "You serious?" He mumbled.

Fly lay on his face, not far from where Stacy continued to sob and wail in between fits of hiccupping. *God. Don't let my luck run out on some shit like this.*

Court frowned at Rabbit and nodded toward Stacy, "C'mon before I get one of my Rottweilers from out back to fuck dis bitch."

Rabbit silently passed Court his 9mm handgun, swiftly dropped his pants, then moved into position behind a helpless Stacy.

"N-n-n-noooo!" Stacy cried out, and awkwardly attempted to scoot forward—burning the side of her cheek against the carpet. "Pleeeeeese Court, don't do me like dis."

"Man, fuck you!" Court snickered as his sidekick struggled and wrestled with a tied up Stacy, as he mounted her.

"Huhhhhh…" Rabbits jaw went slack the moment he entered her sticky slit.

"Pu-leeeeze! God! NOOOO!" Stacy screamed while she was pumped like a stray dog in the middle of the street. She wasn't necessarily screaming from the pain of the assault—it was more from the embarrassment of the despicableness of the rape.

"Yeah, bitch! Yeeee-eah!" he slobbered onto Stacy's bare back as he continued to rapidly slam into her—using his grip on her hips to push and tug her forward and back; like a rocking horse. "Take-dis-DICK!" Rabbit husked and leaned down over her back to roughly shove her head down..

Stacy had gone totally numb. She couldn't feel a thing as her cheek was rubbed raw against the coarse fibers of the carpet. *If I live through this, I'mma kill both of these Niggaz.*

27

"Arrgh! Bitch!" Rabbit exclaimed, discharging inside her womb..

Following the sexual assault, Stacy remained hog-tied on the floor, sobbing as Rabbit's disgusting semen drained between her thighs. Her only option was to wait for a chance to make a move.

"J'yeah!" Rabbit shouted above his victim, while he fastened his jeans, "Dat's how you do dat shit!" His bark though, was actually directed toward Fly.

"Al'ight Nigga!" Court put an end to his boy's boasting and resumed control. He snatched a throw pillow from the sofa as he swiftly moved behind a shuddering Stacy.

POP! PA-POP! Three muffled shots to the back of her head ceased all of her weeping— plunging the room into a deadly silence. Both Rabbit and Fly stared wide-eyed at Stacy lying face-down with a massive hole blown through her forehead.

"Shit." Fly mumbled under his breath. *These young wolves 'bout to murk my dumb ass!*

Unable to pull his eyes away from the brains and skull matter oozing out onto the carpet like scrambled eggs mixed with ketchup and strawberry jelly, Court spoke coldly. "O.G., you know what it is…"

"Look Cuz." In all-out desperation, Fly tried to appeal to their known gang affiliation. "We all left lane Crip niggaz. We don't let no chicks come between us."

Rabbit brought a fist to his mouth and giggled before Court silenced him with an evil glare. "My bad, Cuz."

28

Court shook his head and turned to Fly. "Nah, O.G., you and I both know you can't let dis one ride." A frown creased the corner of his lip. "I caught chu wit' your pants down, literally speakin'."

"Hear me out, doe." Fly had no choice but to try and kick game. "This shit can work to your advantage."

It really wasn't going to change anything, but Court told him to go on and spill his drag anyway. Fly then went on to point out that it would be a very difficult task to carry two bodies out of the house without being seen.

Court chuckled and scratched his ear.

"Hold up... Then you gotta worry about da police or my niggaz from da' Works puttin' this puzzle together..."

"Man, fuck da' Works!" Rabbit blurted.

Fly cut his eyes in the direction of Court's flunky, before coming back to the one who was really running the show. "Look youngen, I fuck with the O.G. Crusher, from over here...real heavy."

Another chuckle escaped Court's lips, "Fly, Crush do run shit. But let's not get it fucked up. He a slime-ball. And, the only reason he fuck with y'all Wilson Works niggas is 'cause y'all so fuckin' deep."

Fly would have shrugged nonchalantly if not for the cords hog-tying him. "I understand all of that. But, nonetheless, our hood's linked."

Court nodded in agreement while scratching his chin, "Aw'ight, I'll give you that. But, what about that other fact?"

What fact? Was the look on Fly's face.

Court grinned devilishly as he read his thoughts, prior to eluding to his point. "Man, you know y'all niggaz over on the Eastside is known for back-dooring fools."

Rabbit jumped in with a suggestion, "We could just burn this crib to the ground wit' dem in it."

Fly did not like the bright glint that suddenly appeared in Court's eyes. "Yo man. The police got all types of C.S.I. shit now-a-days."

"Yeah, I know." Court yawned. "But, I'mma have to take my chances."

Choosing to ignore that last statement, Fly kept on trying. "I can drop a nice piece of change on y'all to make this little situation look like some fools came up in here and pulled a robbery—murder."

"You mean robbery, RAPE, murder." Court corrected him.

Fly blinked a few times to stop the sweat from dripping into his eyes. *I do not like where this conversation is heading.*

"What'chu think?" Rabbit anxiously asked. His eyes seen nothing but dollar signs. "We fuck around and come up."

Court's arms folded across his chest as his head shook from side-to-side, the way a disapproving teacher would look down upon one of their underachieving students. "Nah. This nigga just made me kill my seed. Plus, he'd have us both stinkin' by Tuesday, if we let him walk up outta here." He pointed towards the kitchen. "Rab, go grab a knife."

Fly closed his eyes and began to grind his teeth as Court squatted beside him. "O.G.." He spoke in the calmest of manner. "We need to have a talk about some of that bread you sittin' on."

Chapter 2

The following evening Fly's nephew, Casper, pulled his dark-colored Chevy 454 pickup truck into a parking spot down on a local college campus. He was a strong, wiry built young man with a strange burnt, sienna brown—almost dark orange-ish skin color. He stood a mere 5'7" and usually wore a low, against the grain Ceasar-style hair cut.

Casper was not in a very good mood. He learned that a guy had just run off with a Big Eight. "Homie, that was your fault." Casper cut his eyes at this best friend sitting in the passenger seat. An eighth of a kilo was a significant loss.

"Negative! I ain't takin' that case." Bear pursed his big thick lips tightly and shook his head, "You the one that wanted to front that nigga da' work."

Both young men were a few months shy of their twentieth birthday and had been best friends since the fifth grade.

"Nigga! You the one that said, 'give it to him Cuuuzzzz!'" He mocked the voice of Debo, from the movie Friday, as he came around the truck while putting on his Limited Edition Pelle Pelle, grey and navy blue leather jacket, before pulling his dark skull cap down over his brow.

Towering at 6'5" with the build of an NBA power forward, Bear chose to ignore him while admiring the pearl-blue clear coat he'd painted on the truck yesterday. He adjusted the waist of his extra baggy True Religion jeans, "I like the bowling ball affect it gives to the paint job."

Casper sucked at a tooth, prior to an appreciative grin breaking out on his face. "Miss me wit' all dat. You know the shit hot." He checked the Glock 9 mm tucked in the waist of his oversized Dickies painter pants, as they made their way down the campus' wide walkway toward the main strip that was lined with a number of bars and eateries that stretched for as far as the eye could see.

"Yo!" Bear growled in his deep tone as they noticed three gothic-looking white girls veering their way on an adjacent walkway. He rubbed his large hands together, "Man, I always wanted to fuck a punk-rocker type chick."

Casper smirked and turned to his man. "You got some really weird-ass fetishes."

Truth be told… Bear did have a thing for what some might call, unattractive young women. He always claims to anyone that would listen, that God had blessed those unfortunate in the looks department with beautiful, extraordinary vaginas.

"Cas, you can't always judge a book by its cover."

Casper stifled a chuckle, "See, now there you go with all that philosophyin' shit."

"Nah, I'm tryin' to put'chu DEEEEE!"

He waved him off, "Do you."

As the two young men got closer and closer to the girls, they could see that one of the girls was very tall and walked kind of hunched over with her shoulders slumping.

"Bear, I'll bet'chu the cheese I owe for the paint job, that you can't fuck the tall, Lurch lookin' bitch?"

"Why my shop always gotta be a part of the bets?"

"Fuck it! Put 100 push-ups on it then."

"Nah." Bear frowned. "Bet dat shit. And don't think I forgot about the crash-bar you still owe me for."

"Aw-ight! If I lose, I'll pay double for it."

"Bet!" He pounded his huge fist atop Casper's and then headed for the tall girl and her two petite friends...

"Oh my God!" One of the white girls, Ashley, eked as the two thugs approached them. "I think they're gangbangers." She whispered in her proper, rich white girl tone.

Her equally short friend, Maria, wrinkled her little pug nose. "Ash, stop actin' a fool." Though barely a tad over five feet, Maria displayed the body of a curvaceous swimsuit model, beneath her baggy jeans and other loose-fitting clothing.

Maria and the tall girl, Cidny, were visiting the campus on an unofficial, basketball recruiting trip; while Ashley had tagged along with thoughts of enrolling for the fall semester, to afford herself the opportunity to run wild in the big city.

33

"Hey, how you doin'?" Bear asked the girl that nearly met him eye-to-eye. *Man, she looks a lot better than I thought.* He contemplated, as he took in her smoke-colored grey eyes and her amazing resemblance to WNBA star, Candace Parker.

Cidny lit up. "I'm fine. And you?"

She touched Bear's heart instantaneously the way she mumbled, then bashfully looked down at her toes. Thus he seized on the opportunity. "I'm good. I'm good." He flashed a big, rough-bearded grin and began to talk quietly with her as they strolled down the hill toward Forbes Avenue.

Meanwhile, Casper walked up ahead with the two petite girls. Both girls were well past the point of being pretty in his book and he could tell that the evil looking one had an incredible ass by the way her coat hugged her when the wind blew from their rear.. He went for it by nudging her arm. "So, uh, what's your name?"

Maria seemed to snarl as her green eyes dropped to where he'd just nudged her arm. "Jhu don't know me... so, don't be touchin' me." She offered, with more than enough attitude.

"Aw'ight! Whoa!" He threw his hands up in surrender. "I'm Casper. I was just tryin' to meet'chu."

Her pouty little mouth turned up into a frown. "I didn't ask. Nor, do I wish to know your hoodlum nickname."

Casper bristled at the condescending, white girlish tone she used. "You lil'ass, funky white bitch." He sneared. "Who da fuck you talkin' to?"

Maria wasn't about to back down one bit. She hated everything he stood for. The drug dealing,

34

the guns… his entire thugged-out life style. "What?" She stopped and turned on him. "What'chu gon' do? Pull out jour gun and shoot me?"

He glanced around at the few people looking at them. "Man, you don't even know me."

Her neck snaked and twisted with the effort of her words. "That's what I'm tryin' to tell you. I don't want to know you!"

Casper got in her face and told her exactly how he felt; prior to threatening to make a call to have one of his homegirls come down there.

"Oh, BIG MAN! Jhu gon' have me beat up? Will that make chu feel good?" Maria laughed in his face. "I bet'chu drive a big truck. Or, a car with a big engine to make jhu feel like somebo--"

"No, Maria. Pleeeeease stop!" Ashley sobbed as she tried to pull her friend away from the argument. Her eyes were wide with fear. "We don't know these people." She then whispered, "We could get hurt."

Maria yanked her arm from Ashley with enough unintended force to send her spinning, before she continued to spew hate.. She then pushed a few dark locks of hair out of her face and glared at Casper, "Lee'tle mutha fucker."

He heard the words she gumbled and stepped toward her as if he were about to smack her.

"Oooool! I wish jhu would!" Maria screamed as Cidny grabbed a hold of her from behind.

"What's wrong? What happened?" Cidny whined, while pulling her girl away.

"This fake-ass dude t'ink he know me!" She barked as Bear stood in between her and Casper. "He up here callin' me out mi name."

35

"Okay, okay." Cidny tried to calm down her tempermental friend.

"Pshh!" Casper turned away and looked to the sky. "Somebody betta' get this dumb bitch."

"Jhu fuckin' puto!" Maria hurled back as more people gathered outside around them to see what was going on. "Jhu ain't nu'ting but a LITTLE BOY!"

Casper was seconds from blowing his top when he heard his name fly out of the crowd.

"Lil Reece!" The loud-mouthed female yelled again and elbowed her way through the crowd. "I know you ain't out here talkin' to my lil cousin like you crazy?"

He turned and saw Charrell, one of his sister's friends. "Rel." Casper said in surprise as the stacked young woman walked up on him.

Charrell gave him an evil eye before pushing her palm toward his face in the universal stop sign. She then brushed past a speechless Casper to hug her young cousin, Maria. "Guurrll! You got me down here waitin' on y'all and shit." In her mid 20's, Charrell was a pretty girl from the Wilson Works neighborhood that happened to be extremely protective of her suburban young cousin. "And then, you ain't even answer my calls." She continued on.

Maria checked her phone as they entered the Originals Bar and Grill, "Ooh, my bad." She apologized when she realized she'd been walking around most of the evening with her phone off.

"Yeah, Rel." Cidny remarked while everyone took off their coats to have a seat. "Maria's had a rough day."

36

"What happened?" Charrell asked as she came around the table to give Cidny a hug.

"Some dude up the Student Union touched her ass and she snapped da fuck out!"

"Listen at chu, Cid... talkin' like you from the hood and shit!" She stretched to hug her. "Lean your tall ass down here."

Cidny had to bend over to hug her. "Uhmmm, miss you."

"Me too." Charrell hardly ever got to see Maria and Cidny with them living way out in the affluent, Wexford suburbs. "Uhmm." She pursed her lips following a hug. "So, do we need to go holla at dis nigga?"

"Nah, I took care of it." Maria snarled as she narrowed her green eyes into slits and glared at Casper through the crowd.

Charrell turned her head and followed Maria's eyes—finding them boring an angry hole through the back of Casper's head as him and Bear placed their food orders up at the congested counter. "What happened?"

"Oooll!" Cidny jumped in to describe how Maria had smacked the guy before some of his friends stepped in between them to break it up.. "Yeah, he acted like he wanted to do somethin' until Ashley let it be known who Troy was."

Ashley pushed her shoulders back and sat up in her chair. She felt proud to have stopped the guy in his tracks by blurting out that Maria's brother was Troy, the school's starting middle linebacker.

Charrell twisted her lips into a smirk, "Who's the snow bunny?" She whispered to Cidny, a bit too loudly.

"Oh, I thought you knew Ashley. She went to high school wit' us."

Up at the counter, Casper turned around and leaned back to regard the girls over at their table. It was hard for him not to miss the way Maria's silky black hair flowed from beneath her coal-colored skull cap in curly ringlets. Then she suddenly stood up to reach for a salt shaker on the table next to theirs. *Got Damnnn!* He gaped.

Even in one of her brother's sweat shirts, that was two sizes too big and a pair of baggy Guess jeans, her shapely body remained acutely evident.

"All HELLLLL, NAH!" Charrell rose from her seat to bark at Casper. "Don't be over dere tryin' to ogle her booty!"

Maria looked back over her shoulder and turned up her pug nose before sitting back down. "Ooooh! I hate dat mutha fucker."

Charrell waved her young cousin off and cracked her gun loudly. "Boo, you don't even know him."

"So what!" She said, twisting her neck for emphasis. "I still know I can't stand he'eeem."

Yeah, right. Charrell thought to herself. "Maria, I wouldn't let chu fuck with him anyway."

Her tiny mouth gaped in a silent 'O' as her brow came together in wonderment. "Que quiere decir eso (What does that mean)?"

"For one, he got too many lil bitches all on his dick. And for two..." She looked directly into Maria's eyes. "you aint' fuckin' yet."

Maria could not believe that Charrell had just blew her up in a crowded restaurant. She blinked a few times to clear the haze of anger from her vision. "Why would you…"

Charrell cut her off with the exaggerated rolling of her eyes. "Boo." She chuckled. "Don't act like I ain't keepin' it a hun'ed. SHIT! You should be proud."

Maria began to shake her head, "Al'ight, aw'ight! I'm done wit'it, man. We can talk about it another time."

"Cool." Charrell said with a shrug, which plunged that table into a moment of silence, until Cidny decided to break up the tension.

"Uhh, Rel. What's up with Bear?"

Charrell ran her fingers through her bob-style haircut. "Yeah, you best leave dat nigga alone too. He's just as bad."

Cidny gazed out the huge sidewalk side window, as if something out in the street actually concerned her.

Charrell watched her for a few beats of a second before turning her attention to Maria, who seemed to be slyly observing Casper through the reflection in the picture window. "He ain't gon' do nuthin' but break your heart."

She smacked her lips, "Que (What)! I ain't t'inkin' about he'eem." Maria reiterated that she wanted nothing to do with a dude that had no real direction in life.. "Nada! And he sell dragos. Uh- uh, I'm bien (good)."

Ashley leaned forward and nodded in a show of support for her friend. "Plus, he's kind of dark."

Charrell beheld her like she'd grown a second head. "Ah, what'chu mean by that?"

In a desperate act of pleading, Ashley brought her hands to her breasts. "I didn't mean it like that." She looked to Maria, then Cidny, "I was just saying that he's sooo much darker than Maria."

Charrell left Ashley in a fluster, allowing her to stew in her own mess, while she dipped a french fry into a small cup of ketchup; painstakingly slow. "You know what they say…"

"What?" Ashley asked after too long of a pause.

"The blacker the berry, the sweeter his juice."

The girls sat there ready to burst, waiting for Ashley to catch on..

"Euuuhh!" Maria blurted, "Jhu is naaaasty!"

Tranquilly, Charrell pursed her thick lips. "Ain't nuffin' nasty about it. I'm keepin' it real. SHIT!" She shrugged. "If I ain't have a real nigga like Ja'make, I'd give dat lil nigga a shot of dis snapper." Her bottom lip turned up confidently prior to her adding, "And turn his young black ass OUT!"

The table exploded with girlish laughter as Bear approached with Casper hesitantly in tow. "What ch'all laughin' about?"

His deep voice earned him Cidny's undivided attention. She over-bit her bottom lip and demurely looked away after failing to hold eye contact with Bear—for the umpteenth time that very evening..

Maria sat there steaming. She was ready to blow her top any minute after listening to Cidny tee- hee, purr, and laugh at Bear's every word for the last twenty minutes. "Pshhh!" She huffed out a strong breath and frustratingly pulled off her dark skull cap.

A few seats down on the other side of the table, Casper's dark brown eyes gravitated to the sound. He caught the way Maria tilted her head to the side to smooth back her thick, wavy hair before using one of her wrist bands to tie it into a ponytail. Even though it was clear to him that she was a tomboy type of chick with a bad attitude, Casper could still envision himself bending her over and deep stroking the mean, but cute scowl, right off of her face.

Meanwhile, Charrell sat next to Maria assessing her in a much different fashion. *She is a college freshman and she still dresses like a got damn BOY!* She slightly pondered. *And look at her sittin' there with her damn legs wide open, like a guy with a set of big balls.* Charrell leaned her lips close to her young cousin's ear and spoke, "Gurlll, close your legs."

Maria jerked back and to the side a bit, "Por que (What for)? It ain't like I got on a skirt. I'm wearin' jeans."

"I understand all dat. But'chu 'bout to be dealin' wit college boys now. They gon' be movin' a whole lot faster than them lil rich boys y'all used to dealin' with out there in Wexford."

Casper saw an opening and took a shot. "Yeah, Bear told me y'all from out there. Y'all rich, huh?" He asked as he placed both elbows on the table.

Now dis pendejo (punk mutha fucka) wanna act like we cool? Uh-uh! Maria's lips tightened and her softly squared jaw clenched as she peered down the table..

Cidny knew all about her best friend's temper, so when she saw Maria's nostrils flare, she cut in. "No Casper, our parent's are rich. Not us!" She offered along with a sweet cackling laugh.

41

"Man, so y'all grew up wit' Nannies and shit?" His question earned laughs from all around the table.

"Nah." Cidny shook her head full of sandy-brown curls. "Well, not me. I was an only child until my lil bro came along a few years later."

Ashley put up her index finger, while nibbling at a piece of pizza in her other hand. "I had one."

"I'm sure you did." Charrell sniped and rolled her eyes toward the ceiling.

Cidny attempted to laugh off Charrell's sharp sarcasm by making a joke about Ashley's mother being a trophy wife that wasn't about to change no babies.

"She's right about that." Ashley agreed a bit too staunchly. "All mommy does is spend my father's money."

"T-M-I!" Charrell sniped again.

Bear peeped instantly that Ashley had some mommy issues; thus, he steered the conversation back the other way. "He must got a lot for her to spend, with ch'all livin' way out dere?"

"He do." She sucked at the inside of her mouth. "He's a corporate attorney."

Bear's eyebrows raised, "Aw-ight! He doin' it big." He turned to Cidny. "What'cha pops do?"

She shyly tucked her chin and folded her arms over her mid-section. "He used to play pro football."

"Oh yeah!" He said in amazement. "He played in the NFL?"

"So did Maria's dad." Cidny added.

Maria tensed as the focus moved to her. "Mierda, Puta (Shit, Bitch)! Who told chu to put mi bizness out there?" She squealed at Cidny in a scratchy, raspy whine. "Maldito (Damn'it)!"

42

"Man, it ain't even dat serious." Casper submitted in support of Cidny after she apologized and then sat in her seat like a scolded puppy.

Maria had been itching to spark on Casper since the moment he'd taken a seat at their table — and here was her shot. "Mieda! Tu no se yo (Look! You don't know me)."

He put his hands up in surrender, "Yo, I don't know nuffin' about what'chu just said." Casper decided to try to soften her up. "I can't speak Spanish, but I'd love to learn-"

"Whoa! WHOAAA!" Charrell jumped in, "Casper, don't even think about tryin' to put your THANG down with my lil cuz." She cocked a brow to let him know how serious she was. "Ain't nuffin' jumpin'. PERIOD!"

Another bout of laughter erupted around the table—but this time it was at Casper's expense.

"Haaaaa! Homie, she checked the shit outta you." Bear cupped a hand over his mouth as his deep laughter bellowed throughout the crowded eatery.

"Really, Cuz?" Casper looked to his man like, *Nigga, you supposed to have my back.*

"Aw'ight, aw'ight." He tried to clamp down on the laughing, but when he saw Maria struggling to keep her pouty little mouth pursed tight, he broke into another fit of laughter.

"C'mon, mannnn…"

It took him a few seconds but he managed to get it under control. "My bad, Cas." Bear nodded at Maria and then allowed his gaze to pass from her, back to Cidny. "So, I'm guessing y'all ain't the plain ole rich white girls we thought y'all was? Especially wit' lil Mamacita over here."

Maria allowed a bit of a smile to crease her lips, until she made eye contact with Casper again.

Cidny laid a hand on Bear's shoulder to get his attention, "Her mom's Puerto Rican, but her dad's Black."

"What about 'chu?"

Butterflies explode within her belly with the way he stared commandingly into her eyes. "Uhhhh…" Cidny gasped in a breathless, very unintentional, show of her emotions—earning her a sideways, snarling, green-eyed glare from Maria.

"You Rican, too?"

"No, uh-uh." Her head shook side-to-side. "Black mom, white daddy."

"Al'ight." Bear playfully put an arm around her shoulders. "Got that jungle fever jumpin' off."

"Nah! Uh-uhhhhh." She didn't actually mean to, but when she went to playfully shove him; her hand slid from his chest down to his stomach—prior to her snatching said hand away like a child that had just touched a hot iron.

* * *

Later that night, after using one of the prepaid phones he kept in his glove compartment, Casper sold a quarter key (9 ounces of crack cocaine) to a guy from the South Side of the city. He then went to pick up Carla and took her to a hotel out in the South Hills.. Casper regularly had sex with the 6 or 7 young ladies he kept somewhat close, but Carla had definitely taken the reins and established herself as his girl. She was spoiled rotten. Fine. And thick in all the right places—with the attitude to match…

"Umphh." Carla humphed, slipping Casper's stiff tool from in between her pink lipstick colored lips as she sensually moved her brown body into position to mount him. "Ooooooh." She cooed, "I've been thinkin' about having you deep inside me all day."

Yes, Carla knew exactly what she was working with.

Casper ogled her perky, upturned, chocolate tipped breasts the instant she pushed her shoulders back and thrust them forward. "Hurrgh. Hol-hold up." He twisted at the waist to reach for the brand new box of condoms sitting on the nightstand.

"WHAT!" Carla squawked, "You ain't got not problem splashin' down my throat. But all of a sudden you can't be inside me wit'out a rubber?" She sat astride him pouting like a child.

He showed absolutely no emotion while she went through the bratty dramatics.

"Ooool! You make me sooo sick!" She sneered as she began to get off of him.

"Man, I'm out. Where you want me to drop you?" Casper said, reaching for his pants.

Carla grabbed for the pants and tugged them away from him. "I told chu I'm on da pill." She pled.

Carla and Casper had gone through a pregnancy scare about four months ago, and after dealing with her manipulative childish games, he was in no mood to chance popping one into her oven..

Condom clad, with Carla braced on hands and knees beneath him, Casper mashed her face-first down into the fluffy pillows and commenced to, almost brutally, fuck her brains out for the next few very vocal hours.

Chapter 3

Both of the wide grey metal garage doors, outside of Bear's Auto Body Shop, were pulled down due to the cold weather. Casper parked his black truck halfway up on the sidewalk, beside the vast red brick building.

BOOM! BOOM! After a few pounds with no reply, Casper stepped around a pile of snow and went to the side door entrance.

Last night, there had been a big snow storm. The skies were now cleared, but it was still ice cold enough for the air to burn Casper's throat when he inhaled deeply as he turned the door knob a few times.

"Casper." The bristly white haired man, who unlocked the door, greeted him and moved to the side, as a gust of wind whipped past them.

"How you doin', Pops? Where's Bear?"

Pops eyed Casper over top of the thick glasses perched on his thick pockmarked nose and glanced toward the back office while wiping his hands on a ragged towel he'd pulled from his pocket. "Dey back dere, feedin' them crazy ass piranhas live mice."

With a half of a grin on his usually unsmiling face, Casper ducked around a car raised up on the hydraulic lift before taking a gander further down the line of an old-school Grand Prix in the early stages of its full restoration. He then leisurely continued on to the back office; where everyone usually migrated to when they stopped by the body shop to *kick it.*

"Que paso (What's up)?" Pedro, the best paint sprayer in the shop asked him, as Casper passed in the office doorway.

"You, FOOL!" Casper playfully patted the man's growing gut.

"Si (Yeah)", he chuckled. "Mi wife stuffin' me wit' beans and rice to make sure no other chicas want me."

"And you know you love dat shit!" Casper barked before stepping all the way into the office where a loud group of young boys from the neighborhood—all dressed in big bulky coats and baggy jeans, gathered around the massive fish tank.

"See that one!" Way, a big kid from down the block, eked as a half-eaten white mouse attempted to paddle to the surface. "Got 'em!" The mouse disappeared within a swarm of brightly colored piranhas.

"Bearrrr…" A female voice whined in a high pitch, which caused Casper to turn to see Cidny sitting on the edge of Bear's desk while he leaned back in the high-backed office chair, putting his mack-game down.

"Sup y'all?" Casper's eyes roamed around the spacious office that was more of a Man-cave, than an actual office. "What ch'all up to?"

"Not much." Bear's stout chin jutted toward Cidny. "I'm tryin' to see what's crackin' wit'her doe."

Sheepishly, Cidny over bit her bottom lip and turned to hide her beautiful smile.

Casper shook his head somberly. He watched her perched there on the corner of the desk, looking toothy in a pretty way—and deliciously healthy in her snug fitting jeans, and a heavy hoodie, that did next to nothing to hide the dimensions of her sizeable boobs.. Then a thought came to him, *Bear gon' ruin all of this sweet girls' innocence.* Casper could easily picture some of the scenes from the sexual escapades that had taken place in the office; not to mention, on that very desk. He cleared his throat, "Cidny, where's your lil friend?"

"Huh?" Her smoke-grey eyes blinked a few times then took in Casper's cocky smirk.

"The stubby built one wit' da slick'ass mouth… that said my skin's too dark for her."

She looked at Bear, then back to Casper.

The entire time that Casper watched Cidny give him the *dumb-look*, Bear exaggeratedly shook his head from side-to-side behind her back; prior to him finally just giving up and pointing in the direction of the boys crowding the fish tank.

"Wha-". Casper looked back as one of the smaller boys turned.

Standing in a bowlegged, pigeon-toed stance, Maria snatched the Blow Pop from her pouty little mouth with an audible, *PLOP!* She was dressed like any other young boy from the Wilson Works neighborhood; sporting a dark colored bubble bomber coat over top of a thick hooded sweat shirt, with a pair of acid washed Diesel jeans that were so big that the cuffs nearly covered her itsy, child-sized Nike boots.. "What'chu say about mi boca?"

He looked at her dumbfounded, "Huh?"

She wrinkled her tiny pug nose, snaked her neck and then repeated the words in English. "Mi mouth. Jhu say I gotta slick mouth?" She eyed him from head-to-toe and back up again.

Casper smoothly licked his lips while he checked out the way Maria's shiny black curls snuck from underneath her ribbed skull cap to twirl and twist here and there like ink-colored curly fries. "Maria. Right?" He asked as if he didn't already know her name.

In a rare show of femininity—with her elbow held high; Maria bent her wrist back delicately and even swung the sucker as she spoke. "Si... Yes."

"You know where you at?"

She casually shifted her weight to one foot. "What?" She asked with a shrug of her shoulders. "Jhu gon' go get some girls from around de' corner to jump me?"

Casper did not say a word for a long pause as he gazed around the room at all of the impressionable young faces awaiting his reaction. The last thing he wanted to do was come off looking petty and mean in front of them—because contrary to popular belief, all *street dudes* weren't disrespectful toward their young, Black and Brown sisters. He threw his hands up in a sign of peace. "Yo, chilllll. Why you comin' at a nigga like dat?"

"Nada!" Maria wagged the sucker, and spoke rapidly in that hoarse, scratchy and raspy tone of hers. "Why jhu comin' at me like dat? Chu know jhu was wrong."

He permitted a crooked grin to crease his lips before relenting even further. "Man, you a feisty lil thing."

Relaxed exhalations radiated around the office.

"Ay Cas!" One of the younger boys called out anxiously. "Maria a beast playin' Madden and Black Ops."

"Yeahhh." Casper glanced sideways at the video game system siting on the table before bringing his dark brown eyes back to settle on Maria. "I'mma have to see what's up wit' all that for myself."

"Is jhu…" She maintained a stare just as challenging as his.

"Lil Ron!"

Hearing his name called, he turned to Bear. "Huhhh?"

"Lil homie, I thought you was gon' feed them puppies for me?"

"PUPPIEEEEES!" Cidny bounced her juicy booty up and down on the desk as the youngster tugged up his sagging jeans and headed for the backdoor. "Oooh, Bearrr! I wanna see 'emmmm." She whined, girlishly.

Bear asked Lil Ron to chain up the guard dog, King, and then everyone else filed outside into the barbed-wire enclosed scrap yard where broken down cars and trucks sat in varying stages of dismantlement.

ARFF! ARFFF! The 120 pound German shepherd, King, continued to bark and yank at his hefty chain like he'd lost his mind. Then Mary, the mother of the pups, a large mastiff with a short brindle-colored coat, curiously stuck her head past the rubber flap that covered the heated shack's narrow opening. Spotting the boys and Bear—which usually meant food; Mary trotted out with the puppies in tow across a rough patch of ground checkered with human and dog prints, frozen into the muddy snow.

"Hold-up for a second." Casper. said quickly, as he grasped Maria at the elbow and held her back in the doorway.

Her evil green eyes slowly glanced down at the slight touch. "Que? What?"

He held up his hands in a show of surrender, "Peace offer…"

"Ta'bien." Her ice-grill softened instantly.

Casper titled his head and eyed her.

Maria huffed a humming breath. "It means okay or al'ight."

"Oh, okay. Ta, ta'been…"

She smiled for the first time and displayed a cute, slight gap between her front two teeth. "So, uh, whass'up?"

Casper scratched at the shadowed-down facial hairs along his jaw line. "I, uhh. I wanna take you out to eat or somethin'. Maybe a movie?"

"Uhhhh," Maria looked around before her eyes settled back on Casper. "C'mon nowww."

"What?" He bit at the inside of his mouth and really focused in on her face. He already knew she was pretty--once he got past the tough attitude and her tomboyish ways. *Man, her eyes sparkle like green diamonds.* He mused as he noticed a light dusting of freckles sprinkled across the bridge of her tiny, Minnie Mouse-like nose.

"Casper." Her nostrils flared, "I ain't wit' it."

"What'chu mean?" He was confused. *Is she turning me down?*

Maria glanced out into the scrap yard and inhaled deeply, "Look." She turned to face him. "All jhu wanna do is chalk me up as anotha' una on jour long list. And like I told chu down Oakland de' otha' night..." She peered directly into his dark eyes so that there would be no misunderstandings. "...Jhu- are-not-my-type."

A hard frown overcame Casper's features. "Why? Cause my skin's too dark?" Now, he felt like being petty and mean. It was almost as if her turning him down made him want to hurt her feelings. "It's like, you on some real stuck-up shit."

"Nada!" Maria laughed and then became serious, "Look, man. Chu from here... I'm from there... and it ain't just that." She rushed so he couldn't interrupt her. "I really think that it's wrong to sell poison to our people. I..."

"Who da FUCK is you talkin' to?" He snapped on her. "You don't know SHIT about me!"

A short, heated exchange ensued prior to Maria heading out into the cold with the others.. All along, she had been somewhat dreading another run-in with Casper, every since she'd agreed to accompany Cidny into the city. But after they said what they had to say, it truly hadn't been too bad.

Meantime, farther out in the scrap yard, the mastiff was growing increasingly agitated. Apparently she could scent Maria's female dog on both of the girl's clothing.

Suddenly, Mary gave a menacing growl and charged Cidny, who screamed, dropped the puppy and jumped behind Bear. Consequently, the large mastiff went after an unsuspecting Maria.

"SHIIIIIIT!" Maria darted back past Casper. She ran in a dead sprint over the rocky, snowy ground. But when she realized she would never make it to the door, she veered left.

Like a cat, Maria leapt into the air—practically clearing the side of a broken down minivan as she landed with a *thud* atop its roof. The mastiff though, faltered in her attempt to leap the same distance and slid sideways in the snow. Mary then padded in a circle, barking her head off for a few beats before jumping onto the minivan's hood.

"Mary! Mary!" Bear yelled the mastiff's name over and over, to no avail. Her rage blocked him out as King's crazed barking spurred her on from a distance.

From a prone position flat on her back, Maria cringed at the sight of Mary's sharp fangs as she bounded up on the windshield and snapped at her leg. "No! No! Noooo!" Several times she kicked out at the dog's muzzle, until Bear ran over and yanked the big mastiff off of the car by its collar.

"Maria, are you al'right?" Cidny screehed while helping her to the ground.

"Uh-huhhh." She offered breathlessly, as she gleaned sympathetic looks from everyone except Casper, who seemed to be leering at her.

"Aqui (Here), let me get that." Cidny half-turned Maria.

With an expression of utter hatred plastered on his grill, Casper watched Cidny brush the snow off

Maria's back. Moments earlier during their brief spat, she'd seriously touched a nerve by accusing him of promoting a drug dealing lifestyle to the young boys that looked up to him.. "If it was me, I'd of let Mary bite her." Casper threw his head back and chuckled, "She prob'ly smelt that funky stuff between your legs." He was not affected in the least by the aghast looks that came his way. *Fuck that bitch.*

SPLA-AAAT! "Puneta (Punk-ass nigga)" Maria huffed under her breath in advance of snorting and then hock-spitting into the snow.

Casper stared stupidly at the slimy spit that splattered the snow near the toes of his unlaced Timberland boot. "If dat would-"

"Jhu wasn't gon' do MIERDA (SHIT)!" Maria spewed venomously back as Cidny grabbed her by the back of her coat. "Whaaaat!"

"Bear!" He shouted, "I'm tellin' you. I will smack this bitch!"

"Yo, Cuuzzzz! Chillll!" Bear yelled over his shoulder while he struggled to clip the chain's latch onto Mary's collar.

Casper turned back toward Maria as she continued to curse him out in rapid-fire Spanish. "Bitch! Speak English. I don't understand a word of that shit you screamin'"

Maria sneered and frowned like the word was a bad taste in her mouth. "Ba-Bitch?"

He sneered right back at her, "That's what da fuck I just said."

She yanked away from Cidny and took a step toward him, before thinking better of that course. "No, no, no," Maria shook her head, "Jhu ain't gon' keep callin' me outta mi name."

"Shut da fuck up!" Casper growled pointedly, as he bumped past her on his way back into the office.

Chapter 4

Two days later, Casper and Maria got into it again at Bear's body shop:

Carla entered the body shop's office with her aunt, Ms. Jackie.

"Bear, is my car ready?" The tall, exquisitely dressed, middle-aged woman asked. Her outfit screamed class from head to toe. Through her unbuttoned trench coat, she offered a flash of color-blocked perfection; a black, purple and white patterned Balenciaga dress, paired with black pumps and a hot-pink clutch. Her flawless skin was a deep, rich, pecan brown. And her hair hung to the side in a neat, flowing flounce. Immediately, she detested the young boys sitting around the office watching two of their friends play a video game.. She gently cleared her throat, "Baby, this is not how to run a successful business."

Bear dropped his chin and anguishly rolled his eyes. "I got'chu, Ms. Jackie. Uh, I sent chu a phone message yesterday to come get your car."

"Oh, my bad baby. I got so many fools callin' my damn phone." She said as her walnut brown eyes settled on one little boy in particular. "Where y'all find that little white boy? He's as cute as a button."

Way followed her eyes and took it upon himself to answer, as Maria sat between him and another boy, swiftly working the joystick with her thumbs. "Ms. Jackie, that ain't no white boy. That's a girl." His voice cracked with anxious adolescence.

From her perch on Bear's desk, Cidny cringed.

Ms. Jackie's head jerked back and her raspberry-colored lips tightened. She eyeballed what she now knew to be a cream colored girl sitting between the two boys with a dusky-green skull cap pulled down over her ears. She could see it now. The girl had a strong jaw, but her other facial lines were soft enough to soften it. *Uh-uh.* She could not believe the way the little girl sat there in a pair of oversized Army fatigue pants with her legs gaped wide enough for a truck to drive through. "Uh, hey, little girl." Ms. Jackie spoke in a distinctly motherly tone, "Do you go to school with these boys?"

"No Ma'am. I'mma college student." Maria said as she paused the Dark Ops Video game.

"Ohhh." The woman's penciled in eyebrows raised. She then looked hastily back at her niece, Carla, who confidently clucked her tongue and twisted her fuchsia colored lips.

Maria's nostrils flared in response to the interaction between the two females and Casper. She could not believe that he would actually stand there trying to clown her in front of this *Carla girl*, after he tried to hook-up with her just the other day. But, she wasn't going to feed into it. "Uhmm, I really like jour shoes." Maria offered, sweetly.

"Yeah, thank you." Ms. Jackie gave her a fake, condescending smile and dropped her gaze to Maria's Nike boots. "Unfortunately, Nike doesn't make pumps."

Maria swallowed hard while Carla clipped off a short laugh.

Carla, as usual, was dressed just as stylishly as her aunt; and her attitude projected such. "Bear." She addressed him in a snobbish fashion, without so much as a sideways glance at Maria, or Cidny for that matter. "I'mma wait outside in the car." Her nose jutted into the air, "It smells like dogs up in here."

Casper looked back after Carla brushed him with her hip on her way past him. He admired the rotation of her onion-shaped behind as she allowed a little *something-something* to come into play with her hip movement.. He laughed inwardly because Carla actually knew how to use her hips—and she was one of the few young women he knew that could pretty much keep up with his sexual appetite.

Maria did not realize that she was smirking at Casper the entire time he watched Carla strut her way out the door—until Cidny cleared her throat to get her BFF's attention…

Once Bear left the office to show Ms. Jackie to her car, the second dispute in as many days broke out between Maria and Casper when she refused to hand over his personal joystick.

"Dumb Bitch! Give me the fuckin'-" Casper ducked when Maria threw the joystick at his head, but the length of the cord had snatched it back. He jabbed a finger at her from across the table. "You lucky that ain't hit me."

With all the cockiness of a dude, Maria jutted her soft, yet strong chin forward as she rose from her seat. "What'chu gon' do? Get jour Black Barbie after me?"

He simply stared at her, before permitting a rare smile to grace his dark features. "Don't hate."

Maria's cheeks promptly splashed a deep, beet-red.. Due to her being such a fiercely competitive athlete, with a type-A personality, it was often very hard for her to bite her tongue; thus, her raspy voice trailed off to a mumble, "I could dress like that." She gazed down to her toes and dejectedly added, "If I wanted to."

"Casper." Cidny shrugged off her shyness in support of her BFF. "It's 2004. Maria doin' her."

"Yeah," he snickered. "I'm out."

The patronizing stare Casper laid on Maria before he left the office, cut her deeper than any words he could have possibly chosen to articulate at that moment.

Chapter 5

"Who da fuck!" Casper awoke to the loud ringing of his loft's phone. He reached a wiry strong arm out blindly from beneath the covers. "Yo!" He barked groggily into the phone.

"Casss'perrrr!" Nay-Nay, his sister, sobbed out on the other end. "Oh my God! Casperrrr!"

"Hey! Hey." He sat up in bed, "Nay, what happened?"

She began to hysterically scream that someone had murdered Fly, their uncle.

"What?" Casper yelled back.

"They..."

"Hold up, Nay. Don't say nuffin' else. How far are you from da' loft? Are you drivin'?"

"Ye-Yeahhh..." She sputtered between hiccups.

After instructing his big sis to come directly to the loft before she spoke to anyone else, Casper hung up the phone and sat there on the edge of the bed, scratching his head. *Not Fly, man,* he pondered sorrowfully prior to looking up to see his pit bull,

Master, watching him from the doorway with his intelligent questioning green eyes.

Master shook his head, but continued to hold the eye contact afterwards. It was almost as if he were attempting to read Casper's mind.

"Yeah, Master. Fly's gone."

The dog padded across the rug to lay his big, squared head against Casper's thigh.

Casper lost track of time as he sat in a daze, rubbing Master's head until Nay-Nay arrived. They then went on to sit downstairs on the couch while his sister sniffed and sobbed as she told him everything she knew.

"You sayin' they found him tied up in some pregnant chick's crib, way over on the Westside?" Casper said aloud, more to himself than Nay-Nay. Nonetheless, she nodded as she sat there with Master's head in her lap.

Master blinked a few times and closed his eyes while he instinctively allowed his presence to sooth Nay-Nay.

Meanwhile, Casper frankly could not believe that a seasoned O.G. like his uncle Fly would allow himself to get caught slippin'. "Man, I ain't even know he had a new joint over dere."

"I know..." Nay-Nay sniffed hard and went on scratching the pitbull's ear. "You know that man was a pussy hound."

"Yeah... Ahaaa!"

They both had laughed in remembrance of Fly and his rampant, womanizing ways..

Casper's big sis suddenly sat up, "I keep tellin' y'all niggaz... A fat round ass and a cute face is a niggaz greatest downfall waitin' to happen."

"I know, Nay." He nodded.

She pursed her lips and proceeded to get real motherly with her little brother. "You know, a good shot of coochie has taken down some of the world's greatest empires."

Casper nodded again.

"Boy!"

"Huh?" He flinched at the sound of her sharp yip.

"You hear me?" Nay-Nay could not bear the thought of losing him too.

"Yeah, Nay. Dag, man."

She carried on, undeterred. "You need to slow your young-ass down, too. Quit chasin' every lil girl that's tryin' to give you some of her goodies."

Casper chuckled offhandedly, CRA-AACKKK!

"Boy, I'm serious." Nay replied after smacking her younger brother upside the head.

"Ow, Nay. Damn!" He complained, while rubbing the side of his head. "I told chu. I be usin' rubbers."

Her eyes narrowed into mean slits as Master rose up from her lap and hopped down from the couch to curl up in his favorite spot on the thick dark carpet, beside the black lacquer coffee table. "Casper, you don't listen." She said, sternly. "Usin' rubbers ain't the point! Bitches out in them streets will set chu up for next to nothin'. And don't let some chick you fuckin' have a jealous lil boyfriend. He'll fuck around and wanna bust your head!"

"Man, ain't nooo body gon' split my shit." Casper was just about to launch into more of a rebuttal, when Nay-Nay embraced him with a loving, sisterly hug.

"Mmmmm." She exhaled in relief--while contrarily, the wheels within her brother's head turned with ways of getting things into motion to track down whoever took part in the murder of his uncle.

Casper and Bear were known in certain circles throughout the city, for having an innate thirst for *putting in work.*

"You wearing the chain?" Nay-Nay asked as she felt it's weight against her full, healthy bosom.

Fly had given Casper the heavy, platinum, barrel-styled link chain with the gaudy Casper the friendly ghost character, on his 17th birthday. The three inch long Casper character would dangle down near his stomach when he wore the chain, and it was filled with diamonds. The outside of the white- diamond clustered body was shaded with baby-blue diamonds, while black stones were used to make the eyes and mouth into a sneering smirk.

"Casper, please don't go out flashin' that damn chain."

"I know, Nay. It's under my shirt." He huffed irritatedly.

Nay twisted her lips, "uhm-hmm, niggaz out dere starvin'."

* * *

About an hour later, Casper pulled up in a quiet little tree lined cul de sac and parked his truck in Bear's driveway. He took a quick peek inside his

63

homie's black, fully loaded Hummer before using his key to enter the bachelor pad.

"Whass'up." Bear met Casper just inside the doorway and led the way through the hall, into the living room. "Yo, you see dat peanut butter leather I put in the truck?"

Casper gave him a look that said, *something a lot more serious than new truck interior is going on.*

The bad news made Bear sick to his stomach—he even shed a few tears over Fly's death before the two young men sat down on the couch to crack open a couple of ice-cold 40 ounce beers.

"I'mma miss dat nigga." Bear stated as he passed Casper the half smoked blunt of Purple Haze. "You remember dat time Fly took us to practice for that Pop Warner all-star team? Hu-hughh!" He began to choke on the weed smoke at the same time he tried to laugh. Then he compounded the problem by gulping the Old English malt liquor.

"Ahaaaa!" Casper laughed at Bear, and the memory of that PeeWee football practice. Fly had smacked around two of the coaches because they wanted to keep Bear and him off the team over something that went on in the past with their girlfriends, fooling around with Fly on the side.

"Yo!" Bear howled in his customary, deep low tone. "He smacked da bullshit outta dat one coach. What was his name?"

"Oh, uhh." Casper decided to hit the weed again, when he could not remember the man's name.

"Two hits and pass!"

Casper let the smoke slowly roll from his mouth, as he inhaled it up through his nostrils. "Man, dat shit was crazy that night when you almost spanked (killed) Fly."

"Dat shit kind of funny, now." He said while pinching the tip of the blunt between his thumb and forefinger. "What was we? Like, fifteen?"

Casper nodded as he watched Bear blow smoke toward the ceiling. Bear hit the blunt again and hopped up to act out his story as he told it. "I laid down the mountain-bike by the steps behind yallz old crib." He dropped into a squat like he was Spider Man, "Then, I hear a mu'fucka tryin' to creep through the cut. I'm like, Oooooh! It's 'bout to crack." He moved across the living room in a low crouch, "You know I had that Glock out, Cuz! I was fixin' to start bussin'. Then somethin' told me, Hold up." Bear rose up to his full height and solemnly walked back to the couch.

Casper patted his big friend on the shoulder.

"Cas, I don't know how Big Fly knew it was me. But he whispered my name, right before I started squeezin."

The room became silent for a while, except for the classic NWA track pumping from the speakers.

"Bear." Casper remarked following a few moments of silence. "I am going to murk whoever did Fly like dat."

"Nah, Cuzzz." Bear spoke pointedly. "*We* gon' murder whoever had somthin' to do with pullin' dat move."

Casper nodded, "A'ight, man."

They slouched on the couch and zoned-out to the *old school* gangsta music that Fly loved to listen to. *If I'm not into nothin', I don't feel right. So I grab the nine and da clip and go and murder mutha fuckaz at night.* NWA's Ren spit with venom, as both young men bobbed their heads to the loud, bass enthused killing- season music. *Sayin' they told me but I don't give a fuck! Cause I know my shit is pumpin'.*

RIIIINNGGGG!

Bear's phone rang and he moved with added eagerness to turn down the music and take the call. "Uh, yeah." He then looked away to speak in hushed tones while Casper eyed him skeptically.

"Whass'up, man. Who you talkin' to?" Casper asked as he came around the knee-high table to face him.

Chapter 6

Maria cut her green eyes sideways, at Cidny, as she drove her down the freeway—headed to Bear's house. "I hope jhu know what'chu doin'." She smacked her lips loudly. "Cause there ain't no doubt in mi mind that they sellin' drougas (drugs)."

Cidny smacked her own lips right back and looked out her window. She was really getting sick and tired of Maria's holier-than-thou attitude. "You know what!" She finally snapped back, and mocked her friend's Latin accent. "Jour tio (uncle) sell mucho drogas. And jhu don't seem to have problem wit' he'eeem."

Maria almost laughed, "Puta (Bitch)! Jhu don't know what mi tio do." Then she added, "Pluse, I ain't fuckin' mi tio."

Cidny's eyes got as big as saucers, as her skin flushed with guilt.

"Ooooo! Ooooh!" She hooted, between cracking her gum.

Cidny grumbled without much conviction. "Maria, stop playin'."

Ignoring the plea, Maria went right on teasing.

"For reeeeal." Her grey eyes began to fill with tears. "I think I might love him."

"What?" Maria hissed, causing the VW Bug to pitch to the left a little before she got it back under control.

Cidny hoped and prayed that Maria wouldn't say another word while they rode in silence. She knew if her BFF looked into her eyes she'd burst into tears.

"I really-really hope jhu know what jhu are getting' jour self into." Maria warned while keeping her eyes on the road. She hit the turn signal and turned right, onto the South exit ramp.

After so many years together, Cidny had become accustomed to Maria's sometimes abrasive attitude. Thus, she titled her head back and closed her eyes. She thought about how close her and Bear had become in such a short amount of time. They would talk on the phone for hours on end; talking about any and everything—even the subject of an experimental time in her life when she'd wondered whether she were straight or gay.

Cidny's recollection of the chance and then subsequent encounters were still very lucid in her mind, *the young lady by the name of Sue had been a star basketball player at Wexford High before going on to star at a small college in the middle of the state.*

Over the summer, Sue began to work with Cidny to help her improve her agility and low-post moves that would assist her with receiving better scholarship offers. And so it came to pass one evening following a particularly grueling workout. Cidny stepped into the showers and commenced to soap up her curvesome, young, sexually inexperienced body--while Sue talked with her boyfriend on the office phone.

Cidny knew they had the entire gym to themselves since it was their responsibility to lock-up at night. So, due to some heightened horniness from such a brutal session, she decided to get a quickie off within the privacy of the showers. She used her loofa to stroke her already stiffened clitoris and choked off a sensuous moan by hissing a long breath of air through her flared nostrils, almost as if she were a big mare in heat. "Huhhh!"

Cidny gasped in surprise at the sudden appearance of Sue, in the nude, stepping from the shadows into the showers. "Nuhh…"

"What'cha doin', Cid?" The towering brunette was built similarly to Cidny, except in the hips and booty department. "Shhhh… No need to answer." She began to kiss her startled friend's plump, 36 Double D's; flicking her extremely long tongue over the erect nipple. "Mmmm, these remind me so much of my own big boobies." She cooed.

Cidny proceeded to murmur the most pleasurable sounds to Sue's ears as her experienced tongue trailed its way down over the aggressive swell of Cidny's hip, into the V of her thighs.

"Wuhh-huhh!" She cried out the instant Sue's tongues plunged inside her sticky nest.

"Uh-uhmmm." The woman mewled as her young conquest squirmed in her strong hands. She held Cidny where she wanted her; allowing her hungry mouth to feast voraciously on her frothing creaming sex.

Feeling the explosion arise from deep down in her belly, Cidny cried out even more passionately while bucking against Sue's sucking mouth. The euphoria of cumming harder than she'd ever cum in her young life caused her to lose her ability to stay upright. "Uhh!" She went slumping into the embrace of a smiling Sue.

"Here, here." Sophisticatedly, Sue comforted her, caressed her. *I think I need to show her some of the games the college girls like to play,* the white girl mused.

Sue slid back on her knees, forcing a spent Cidny to slip from the embrace, forward, onto her hands and knees—leaving her profoundly vulnerable, in a face-down, ass-up position as the shower's soft steamy spray pelted her back.

"Hmmmm." Sue hummed while admiring the sight of Cidny's glossy, marbly, abounding rump from behind. Languidly, she licked her already creamy lips as she contemplated just where to begin..

"Oool-uhhh, nuhhh." Cidny sobbed moments later as she tried to wriggle out of Sue's strong grasp.

Initially, Cidny's untutored body knew-not how to react to a tongue licking her in such a deplorable, shameful place. However, she was soon lustfully rolling her shapely rear-end back, onto the skilled tongue assaulting her puckered little nether aperture.

"Ooooh, fuck! That's right. Lick my ass!" Cidny panted and howled as the beginnings of an assgasm struck her.

Sue took the unabashed movements and utterances as a cue to spread her young friend's cakes apart even more, which allowed her long talented tongue better access.

Following the shower episode, Cidny and Sue began to hookup regularly—until Sue's boyfriend happened to stumble upon them one evening inside the gym's locker room, engaged in a very compromising situation. He gave Sue an ultimatum on the spot; and without a second thought, she chose him.

"Mieda (Hey)!" Maria snapped Cidny out of her daydream.

"Oh, uhh, huhh?" She quickly shook off the daze.

Maria gave her girl a second look. "Damn, dat nigga got jour cabeza (head) in de' clouds."

Cidny simply shook her head and got her book bag from the backseat.

"Jeah! Jour welcomed." Maria barked before putting the cute little car into drive.

* * *

Inside the house, Casper was in the middle of berating Bear for his decision to have any female—let alone one he'd just met; to have knowledge of where he laid his head.

Bear shrugged his wide, huge shoulders. "I'm feelin' her."

"What!" Casper was about to go all in on him, when the doorbell rang. He gave Bear a disapproving glare, "I'm surprised you ain't gave her a key, yet."

Cidny came prancing into the living room ahead of Bear—until the sight of Casper standing in the room caused her to fumble her steps in a guise of uncertain shyness.

Casper noticed the way her entire demeanor changed. "Sup?" He offered in an attempt to break the ice, "Cid, right?"

"Uh-huh." She seemed to relax some, but she still folded her arms across her full breasts and regarded him with skeptical grey eyes.

He took note of Cidny's long, extra baggy basketball shorts. Her big, thick hoodie. And her unlaced, retro, Charles Barkley quarter inch Nike's. "What, you comin' from hoopin'?" Casper asked in a joking manner.

Cidny seemed to emerge from her shell as she threw her wide shoulders back and raised her chin. "Me and my girl, Maria, was just down the Pete, runnin' ball wit' some of the local college girls."

"Yeahhh." He was more than a little impressed, "Y'all got game like dat?"

"He'll tell you." She jerked her thumb back at Bear as he entered the room. "He came to see two of our games already."

"Ohh, yeah." Casper gave his boy an accusing eye.

Cidny disregarded the look between the two and went on, "We're the top ranked players in the state, according to pretty much all of the recruiting websites."

The way Bear stood there with a big dumb grin on his face, like a proud pop; wasn't lost on Casper..

Cidny had dropped her bag at the bottom of the steps and took up a seat on Bear's lap. She gave him a look with those smoke-grey eyes before he even thought about trying to protest in front of Casper. *Act funny if you want to.* She said with her eyes, then gripped his 40 and downed the rest of it.

Casper had to admit to himself that he liked her.

"I'll get'chu another one." She hopped form his lap and daintily stifled a burp, "You want one too, Casper?"

"Uh, ahh, I'm cool." He tried with all his might, not to look at the abundance of ass she presented—even in a pair of oversized basketball shorts; as it bounced out of the room.

Casper, Bear and Cidny, sat in the living room, *kickin' it*, for close to an hour, prior to her heading upstairs to shower-off the sweat from playing ball.

"Bear, I'm out." Casper said, before Cidny had cleared the top step.. What the two were about to get into, was not a mystery to him. "Can I use your bike?"

"Of course. But'chu gotta pick it up from the shop."

"A'ight." He said on his way out the door.

"And, don't do nuffin' wit'out me!" Bear barked, just before the door shut.

Chapter 7

The CRB 1100's powerful engine revved, as Casper cruised on the bike, through the Westside neighborhood where Fly had been found, tortured to death. The neighborhood was much the same as his own, except for the two huge public housing developments. The blocks looked eerily the same with rowhouses, some in better shape than others, stretching the length of most blocks—with hidden cuts that cut across blocks like a ragged ghetto maze to connect the streets to the even more dangerous alleys.

Due to a break in the cold weather, hand-to-hand sales in the open-air drug market were in full swing. And, there was an abundance of fine young brown bunnies out and about, looking to catch themselves an emerging *money-getter*.

Even though he'd spotted a few prospects, Casper kept the visor down on his helmet. He was over on that side of the city for work, not play. He was scouting the area that he would soon be doing some hunting in. "Huh." He rode up on the curb and drifted around to the back of a gas station to answer his vibrating phone. "Yo!"

"Dat ain't how you answer no phone!" Nay-Nay eked in his ear.

Casper removed the phone from his ear and stared at it in his hand. "Who you talkin' to?"

She basically ignored him and continued on with what she had to say. "Stop pass da' house, ASAP!"

"What!"

"Look boy! Rell came through with dat."

"Say no more." Casper hopped back on the Freeway and shot over to his side of the city in half the time that it would normally take. He knew how meticulously Charrell went about gathering information from her job down at the Department of Energy. She would have addresses, a list of the children living in the home, and even a brief description of the young woman whose name appeared on the lease; including notes on how she carried herself, along with her work hours if she happened to hold a job.

The next morning, Casper sat alone inside of a stolen Bonneville, parked in the middle of a trash strewn block on the city's Westside. He could not wrap his head around the word on the street that Court and Rabbit had played a part in Fly's death.

"Them niggaz betta hope da' police catch up to 'em, before I do." He groused while his leather clad fingers gripped and re-gripped the steering wheel.

Casper had been somewhat cool with Court and Rabbit during their time together, locked-up in the George Jr. Prison for Youth Offenders. And now he sat patiently out in front of the rundown rowhouse of a hoodrat that Rabbit was known to stay with from time-to-time. He really wanted to catch up to Rabbit first, because with him not being the brightest bulb in the box, Casper hoped that he might put him onto Court's whereabouts without realizing he was actually doing it.

While watching the rowhouse, Casper's mind began to drift to stories he'd heard about Fly from back in the middle 90's—when he put together a *powermove* and became the first bigtime coke dealer to start selling powder cocaine instead of crack. It was often said that Fly was a thinker that was ahead of his time, so when he changed the game and began to sell powder to avoid the 1 to 500 gram ratio; comparing crack sells to powder sells in terms of prison sentencing guidelines, he also struck deals with his high volume clients to teach them his personal crack-cooking recipe that used a handheld whipper and a few secret ingredients to whip-up one kilo into almost two, much more potent kilos. "Shiiiiit!"

Casper snapped from his reverie, just in time to spot Rabbit cautiously ease down to the broken sidewalk from the shadows between two adjacent rowhouses.

Rabbit pulled up his saggy jeans with one hand as he hopped from the curb with a bit of pep in his step, while Casper slid from the car to follow from a safe distance.

A few blocks later, Rabbit went inside of a small corner store which gave Casper a chance to pause and develop a plan to his rapidly evolving dilemma. Casper never envisioned in a million years that he'd actually run into Rabbit or Court on the first day of hunting..

This type of shit never moves dis fast. Casper mused while leaning against the wall outside the store, with the bill of his ball cap pulled down. He began to allow a number of potential scenarios to play out in his head. First thing first, he needed to ask Rabbit a few questions that would surely not get answered if he was lying on the ground with bullet holes all in his body. Second, there was the matter of his own safety. Casper knew that Rabbit would definitely be strapped. Ready for it. Looking for it.

Rabbit exited the store in a bowlegged-waddle to keep his pants from falling down under the weight of the cannon tucked in his waist band.

Casper kept his head down as Rabbit walked right past him, as he downed some sort of drink he carried inside of a brown paper bag. Silently, Casper slid up behind his unsuspecting target and jammed the gun barrel into his back. "Hey." he growled the way a cop would, and grabbed a hold of Rabbit's Polo coat collar with his free hand. He then ushered him into the narrow walkway in between the store and an abandoned neighboring building.

Rabbit silently cursed himself for not minding his P's and Q's. He knew he was supposed to check, and re-check his immediate surroundings in times like this. "Wha-Whass'up?" He gurgled out through a mouthful of malt liquor.

"On your knees, Loc." Casper ordered from behind, ending the charade that he was a police officer.

Rabbit cursed under his breath, threw the beer down into all of the other trash around them and knelt.

"Put your hands on top of your head and lace ya fingers." Casper instructed, "Now, turn. Hey!" He tapped the back of his head with the barrel. "Turn real slow. Don't make me pop your top."

Rabbit followed the orders that led to him peering up into the dark hole of a 9mm, held by none other than a Loc he knew from Eastside Wilson Works. "Uh-uhh, Ca-Casper?" He stammered, "'Sup, Ca-Cuuzzzz!"

Rabbit's high-pitched whine immediately left a bad taste in Casper's mouth—just by the way his voice changed in that split second, he knew Rabbit played a part in what happened to his uncle. But regardless of that, he still needed to line him up. "Rab, I know Court did Fly. I don't see you violatin' no O.G. like that, unsanctioned that is."

"Right! Cuzzzz." Rabbit seen the opening and went for it. "I told dat nigga! I was like, Yo dude official. Don't do it!"

Casper nodded in agreement with his version of the story. "Look doe. I'mma need to know where dat nigga layin' his head… Right now!"

Already contemplating how and where he was going to pay Casper back for making him piss himself, Rabbit gave up his homie without a second thought. He'd been getting bad vibes from Court anyway. Plus, he knew his homie's penchant for getting loose ends out of the way. *Why not backdoor him, before he backdoors me?* He thought with an inward shrug.

Meanwhile, Casper could not believe how easily Rabbit gave up Court's duck-off (hideout) spot. And he was almost positive that the information was correct, because he remembered the name Nicky from Charrell's notes. *She should be at work, too. Man this shit is going too damn perfect.*

"Casper, I'm tellin' you. That-nigga-is a snake. I watched him murder his own, unborn kid."

"Rab," He looked calmly into his eyes. "He tortured my uncle?"

Rabbit's eyes dropped down to the garbage littering the ground. "I ain't sure, man. I bounced after he buss' his baby momma's head." He looked up with pleading eyes. "He was still talkin' to your uncle when I left."

"Yeah, a'ight Cuz." Casper exhaled in relief, "I'mma try to catch up to this fool. I know how you rock. So, turn back around 'til I get up outta here."

"Awww, mannn." He released a whinny whimper as he shuffled around on his knees to face the opposite direction.

"Loc, I ain't got no beef wit'chu. Just stay facin' dat way 'til you count to like, forty." Casper picked up a discarded two-liter plastic bottle as he spoke.

"You ain't gotta worry 'bout me. I don't' even fuck wit' Cuz no more." Rabbit was just waiting for Casper's feet to shuffle through the trash, then he planned to start blazing. "Real talk, I might-" He was milli-seconds away from reaching for the cannon tucked in his waist when, PA-pop! to the back of his head.

Casper fired through the opening at the top of the plastic bottle and blew a hole through Rabbit's forehead that sprayed the cluttered walkway with a grotesque mixture of blood, brains, and small off-white jagged shards of skull.

Casper did not wait around to admire his wet work. He slithered swiftly from the narrow walkway unseen, unheard, and unassumingly walked back to the Bonneville—which was no longer there. The stolen car had been re-stolen, forcing Casper to head out on foot in the direction of Court's girl's house, which was no more than a 10 minute run for him.

As he settled into a brisk pace, his mind began to calculate a few strategies; and he realized that he would need a ride back to the East side of the city..

"Aye Bear." Casper spoke into his cell as he continued to run on the mostly uneven and broken sidewalk, "you still laid up wit' Cid?"

"Fuck you, nigga. I'm at da' shop." Bear was quiet for a moment or two, then he began to retaliate. "Yo! Don't take shots at me, 'cause Maria made you look dumb the other day."

"What man! Fuck dat Gwalla-Gwalla speakin' bitch." He was still pissed off over the way Maria clowned him in front of the entire body shop. "I wasn't even tryin' to get with her. I was just tryin' to be friendly."

"Yeah Nigga. Keep it a hun'ed. You tried to spit game and she flea'ed you."

Casper hopped over a missing, snow-filled section of the sidewalk and barely broke stride. "Look man, later for all dat. I need you to come scoop me."

"What…" Bear seemed to pay closer attention to the call, "Is you runnin'?"

"Huh?"

"Nigga, you heard me." He griped. "You went and hollered at them bitches, didn't you?"

"Listen homie…"

"Nah man. Fuck dat! And fuck you." Bear barked.

There was a long, tension filled silence before Casper finally spoke. "Bear, is you gon' come get me or not?"

"Pshhh! Where you at?"

He instructed Bear to pick him up in the parking lot of a McDonald's that sat on the corner of 9th Street, just off of the West End exit of the Freeway.

"A'ight, man."

"C-40 (Come careful)!" Casper added quickly before hanging up. He knew it was a risk to make this move on foot; however, he felt like he needed to press the issue prior to word of Rabbit's murder reaching the street.

"Yeahhh." Casper steadied his breathing and pushed himself harder. *I gotta catch up to Court before he goes underground.*

Casper loved to workout and run—him and his pit bull, Master, would sometimes run the trails down by the river for hours. During those runs Master liked to dart off into the brush to chase squirrels, cats and who knows what else. But all-in- all, to Casper, he was the smartest dog in the world. It was as if he followed instructions like a human.

Master had moved in with Casper a little over two years ago, after Mr. Willy, his initial owner, was murdered by Federal agents when he was still a puppy. Mr. Willy was an older, cool, somewhat crazy dude that had lived down the block from Casper's grandmother since forever. He was also a Gulf War veteran that had been paralyzed by friendly fire during the conflict; and he never lacked for stories to tell

Casper when he used to sit on the man's stoop as a kid—in between runs to the corner store for Mr. Willy's cigarettes, sodas and whatever else the well paid errands entailed.

However, as Casper grew older he learned that Mr. Willy had a deep-seeded hatred for the government he once served, because of the government's policies towards helping injured Vets like himself. Thus, to make ends meet, Mr. Willy kept watch over a safe that Fly cemented into his basement floor.

As Casper began to sample more and more of the street, his time hanging out with Mr. Willy greatly decreased. However, he would still drop by from time-to-time to *kick it* with the old dude; and that's when he first encountered the small, green eyed pit bull pup with the white chest and white socked paws.. Mr. Willy would always show-off Master's intelligence on those visits by having the pup do things like; go up stairs and get his slippers, go find his wheelchair racing gloves, or go get his bag of Puppy Chow and drag it into the living room. Then, about three months after Willy got the puppy, the D.E.A. smacked his crib and he came out inside of a body- bag following a brief gun fight.

Later that day, Casper sat on the steps leading to Nay's porch with his head buried in his hands while nearly the entire block protested down the street, out in front of Willy's house. He could hear all of the screaming and shouting as he sat there reminiscing on the good times with his old-head, when he abruptly looked up and spotted the puppy trotting up the opposite side of the street with his oversized head swinging back and forth like he was looking for something or someone.

Casper jumped up and shouted, "Master!"

The small pup's ears stuck straight up, he looked both ways then came scurrying across the street so fast that his body veered sideways and he just about fell over.

Chapter 8

Casper had begun to huff some, as he neared Nicky's small split-level white home. He'd already decided during the run that the best way to enter the house would be through the backdoor.

Meanwhile inside the house, Court, a brown-skinned, handsome young man whose build mirrored Casper's, stepped into the shower with his trusty 9mm handgun after pounding Nicky's sticky kitty kat for the better part of the early morning. Subconsciously, he'd been spilling his seed inside of her several times a day, in an attempt to make a child to make-up for the one that he'd murdered.

Stealthy, Casper entered the kitchen through the rear door—missing Nicky by mere moments as she rushed out the front door, late for work. Casper knew that he should have checked the house better, but the notes said there were no children; and when he heard the shower running upstairs, he just had to take another gamble.

He could clearly hear Court rapping to an old Tupac joint playing over a small radio, as he listened from outside the open bathroom door. "I can make a mu'fucka, shake, rattle and roll." He rapped on-and-on while Casper removed his chrome SIG 9mm from its spot atop the toilet seat.

With Court's gun in hand, Casper crept down the hall to the bedroom, "Whew!" He blocked his nose with his forearm to ward off the smell of funky sex permeating the room. He then snatched a pillow from the bed and went back to the bathroom.

Casper forcefully yanked down the shower curtain and hopped back. "Sup Court?"

There was a very long pause before Casper winked and raised the pillow with Court's SIG behind it. Booph! Boophh! the muffled blasts exploded through the pillow in a puff of flying feathers. The first two shots struck Court in the stomach, slamming him up against the shower wall as the preceding shots peppered his chest and torso with silver dollar sized holes. Casper then ended it with a blast to Court's forehead and a blast into his left eye.

Casper did not even realize the pillow was on fire as he watched Court slip soundlessly down the tiled wall—dark blood bubbling from the hollow socket where an eye had once been. "Oh shiiiiit!" He flung the gun and the burning pillow into the sink and took one last look at Court slumped in the bath tub in advance of going back into the smelly bedroom where he wiped his own gun clean before stashing it under the mattress.

Casper really hated to be on the wrong side of the city without a gun. Especially after he'd just killed two members of the Westside Trackstone Crips. *I know it's better to get caught with a strap, than without one. But fuck gettin' grabbed with a joint that got a fresh body on it.* He deduced as he exited Nicky's crib just as stealthy as he'd entered. He then tucked his leather gloves into his back pocket and strolled very nonchalantly down the squalid, grimy back alley.

* * *

"What's up, Big Homie?" Casper asked jovially as he jumped into the dirty Buick with Bear, who simply glared. "Whose car is this?"

"Nobodies." Bear answered flatly.

He knew his man was mad. "Cuzzo, I had no idea I'd run into them dudes."

"I ain't tryin' to hear all dat, man. You did what'chu did."

"Bear." He tried to plead his case. "I was just doin' some surveillance, and them niggaz fell in my lap."

He looked out his window and shook his head. "You got a lotta' shit wit'chu."

"It wasn't planned." Casper mumbled around the fries he'd stuffed in his mouth.

The car became quiet once Bear accepted a Quarter Pounder from the McDonald's bag and drove out of the parking lot.

"Aye." Casper spoke after they'd rolled down the Freeway for a few minutes. "I'mma take that 72 hour rule up a notch."

Bear gave a look that said, *Go on.*

"Until some heat go down, I'mma go visit my uncle Harold."

"Way out in Kansas?"

"Yeah." Casper gazed out the window. "You got a clean ride for me wit' da' paperwork?"

"Shit, you can take dis one."

If there was actually a book on "Body Snatching", there would surely be a section that advised you to disappear for at least 72 hours after committing a murder.

Chapter 9

Headed west, Casper had the car on cruise control while his boy, Master, sat in the passenger seat watching the sights pass by. He seemed particularly interested in the farms and the occasional grouping of livestock that milled and moved about here and there along the interstate.

"You wanna eat one of them cows, huh Boy!" He reached over to rub the back of the dog's head.

Master barely took his eyes off his window to acknowledge Casper. He simply made a whining sound and slipped his pink tongue out of the side of his mouth.

Casper took the hint and settled in for the long drive. He began to think back to that eventful morning as he drove and Master curled up on the seat to nap. *There was Rabbit, face down in that narrow walkway with his brains spilling out of his cracked open skull. Then there was Court, staring back at him with one of his eyes nothing more than a dark, blown-out hole where the eyeball had been.*

It was as if something clicked in Casper's head that made him think, *do I still want this life?*

* * *

Two days after Casper left town, a meeting was scheduled inside the conference room of the Major Crimes Unit. Chief Homicide Detective Larsen was drinking a bitter cup of coffee, while standing outside the room. As usual, he took his *good ole' time* before entering the stuffy area. He had the look of an old, beaten down former boxer with saggy bags under his sickly looking eyes. He was also a very mean, vindictive man that drank and smoked, way too much.

"Okay!" Larsen yelled as he stepped authoritatively into the room. He was not too happy to see a week go by without a single arrest warrant being issued for any of the four homicides that had taken place on the city's West side. His mean, red eyes took a slow pass around the meeting room, daring anyone brave enough to even try to hold his gaze.. "All youz pieces of SHIT!" he bellowed, "I want some fuckin' solid leads. Now!"

The entire room seemed to flinch and shudder. Then a tall black officer looked at his white, psychopathic partner and rose slowly from his seat.

"Uh-hmmm, Sir." Officer Johnson cleared his throat as his partner continued to sit quietly in his seat.

"What'cha got?" Chief Larsen glared while wondering whose sick joke it was to pair up an ass-kissing nigger with a retarded redneck.

89

"As you know, Sir, one of the first two victims was a Billy Smith." Johnson glanced down at his note pad. "His nephew, one, Reece Alvarez Smith, is a known shooter, who, me and my partner once put away for murder a few years back. Well," he said in a huff. "That was before his uncle managed to use some of his considerable drug earnings to get the conviction overturned-"

"Hey, hey!" Larsen cut him off. "Get to the fuckin' point."

"Yes Sir." He swallowed his pride, literally, and went on. "We believe that the second of the two murders were committed in retaliation, by the nephew, Reece-"

Chief Larsen cut off Johnson even more rudely than the last time. "Look! Trust me. I know you got a hard-on for that little half-breed nigger, Mexican or whatever he is. No offense."

"None taken, Sir." Officer Johnson replied proudly.

Larsen used an agitated wave of his hand to shut up the black officer, "Just bring me something, so we can put his ass away for good this time."

"I promise you, Sir. I will... By any means necessary-"

"No, no, no!" He put up his hands to stop him. "I don't need to hear all of that."

"Sorry, sir."

* * *

Another week or so following the murders, a tall muscular young man named Grieve, who happened to be Court's older brother, stood out in front of one of the three Trackstone highrises. At the present, he was one of the project's most feared young wolves.

Grieve swelled his chest with a deep breath as he looked toward the cloudy grey sky. He then looked out at the lowrise units that spread out beneath the three highrises like square rocks, scattered beneath tall trees. The Trackstone Housing Development was its own city inside of a city with its numerous illegal businesses thriving within its borders. Besides the bustling drug trade; there was an old school bus parked in the center of the project that had been converted into a bodega that sold everything one would find inside of a convenience store. There were also apartments throughout the project that sold anything from stolen designer clothes, shoes and bags; to some of the finest jewelry that money could buy.

Now Grieve, a thug's thug that acquired a serious herion habit during his last prison stay, loved the Trackstone's brutal environment in which the strong preyed on the weak. "Yo! Look out, lil nigga." He pushed a smaller dope seller to the side as a potential sale approached.

"'Sup Grieve. I'm tryin' to grab a quarter of hard (cooked cocaine)." The linebacker-sized woman asked.

He arched one brow, "Truck, I know you ain't smokin'?"

"Fuck NO!" She shrieked and turned to the side to give him a view of her wide, somewhat flat, booty. "Nigga, I'm fresh out da' County!" Truck paused long enough for Grieve to catch the hint—which he didn't. She then broke into a smile that exposed a huge missing front tooth, before leaning forward to whisper in his ear. "A bitch ain't got hit in 6 months."

He released a long, drawn-out, "Ohhhhh."

A now 23 year old Grieve had been secretly having sex with Truck since he was 14 and she was 21.

"C'mon gurrlll!" Grieve said moments later as he led a very reluctant Truck around to the back of the highrise.

"I'm tellin' you. I'm not fuckin' in nobody's pissy-ass stairwell."

"Why you trippin'?" He grabbed her by the wrist and pulled her toward the door. "Man, we pay crazy-ass Bob to bleach these joints."

At first, Grieve wasn't even planning to have intercourse with her because his brother's old girl, Nicky, had taken his man down twice already that morning. But after he thought about it, he could not pass up the chance to dig out Truck's amazing shot, first.

Not to be a meta-cognitive (thinking about your own thinking) in regards to Grieve's rational, but the fact that he'd been fucking his dead brother's girl since the funeral, did not seem to faze him in the least.

"Hmm! Ahh! Ye-yeahhh!" Grieve's muffled, labored grunts and groans filled the 3rd landing of the dimly lit stairwell as Truck bent at the waist and pressed both hands flat against the wall.

"Ooooh-ooooh! I-can't-belieeeeve I'm lettin'-chu-do-me-like-thissss." Truck husked lustfully and pushed her wildly churning rearend back to meet the slamming thrusts assaulting her from behind. "Dat's riiiiight!" She hissed and looked back. "Feed-me-that one eyed monster!"

They were some sight! Grieve had his sweat pants pushed down to his ankles to gather around his tightly laced prison work boots; and Truck was begging for more, before quickly pleading for a little less.

Ten minutes later, Truck left the building through the front while Grieve exited out the back. She was feeling pretty good after getting her back blown out and coming up on a whole onion (1 ounce of crack) instead of the quarter ounce that she had come for. Truck had plans to catch a cab over to the Southside to meet up with the little white girl she'd protected down the County Jail for the last few months. She felt that this would be her chance to go and make some fast money in a spot that nobody really knew about it.

Meantime, in need of treating his nose, Grieve rolled up on a young hustler pitching stamp bags of heroin on the side of the highrise. "Easy, let me hold a bag?"

"I just sold out, Loc."

As Grieve stared down at Easy, debating whether or not to run the youngsters pockets, an older dope-fiend seized what he thought was an opportunity. "Grieve." He tapped the breast pocket on his dingy blazer. "You can get on this bag with me."

"Whaaaaat!" Grieve backhanded the man with so much brunt force that he went sprawling head over heels. Then, as the man curled into the fetal position, Grieve really spazzed. He commenced to kick and stomp the old man to death.

Chapter 10

Following a challenging workout with her mother down in the basement gym, Maria stood in front of her bedroom's full length mirror after a very long, self-satisfying bubble bath. Even though she remained a virgin, her insatiable sexual itch had her engaging in forms of masturbation before she was old enough to know what she was doing.

Maria turned to the side and placed a hand on her washboard stomach, as she observed the explosive curves that anyone other than herself would look at as a gift from God. Her waist measured at a ridiculously narrow 24 inches, accenting her voluptuous hips and highlighting a protruding, almost cartoonish round butt. Then, there were her thick, slightly bowed, strong athletic legs that led down to a pair of the tiniest, pigeon-toed feet.

Her lips twisted as she cupped, then weighed a set of boobs that favored a couple of swollen, ripe grapefruits. Maria's 34D's sat up proudly, with or without a bra—her mother had once joked about passing her daughter a set of cursed nipples that constantly appeared in a state of arousal, poked out and pointing like bullets.

In frustration, Maria turned away from the mirror and began to dress in an old, comfortable pair of sweats that covered up the body issues she'd been dealing with since the 6th grade.

Despite Maria's body issues, she had a closet full of the latest fashions after going on a pre-college shopping spree up and down the Eastern seaboard, under the constant tutorial guidance of a mother, who she used to play dress-up with as a toddler—modeling and strutting around the house like a miniature peacock in the specially made high-heeled shoes her mother bought for the pageants Maria would never partake in once she followed her older brother to a few practices and fell in love with athletics—and began to trail him around like a shadow, doing push-ups, throwing balls, as she became a rough and tumble tomboy..

Maria flicked absentmindedly through the channels before deciding to sneak downstairs to raid her brother Troy's secret porn stash.. She wasn't even halfway there when she realized there was no need to sneak, due to the sounds coming from her parent's room. She smiled because when she was a kid she used to sneak peeks through that very keyhole. *God, what was wrong with me? I must have been a lee'tle freak.*

* * *

Deep inhaling and exhaling filled the otherwise quiet bedroom as Bear and Cidny lay atop the gigantic-sized bed, with their sexually sated limbs intertwined while they rested.

Cidny reveled in how good it felt to press her left cheek against Bear's broad sweaty chest. Then she interrupted the moment, "Bear, when do you think Casper's coming back?"

"Huh?" Her question caught him off-guard as he lay there idly wirling a wild lock of her sandy-brown hair around his index finger. "Where did dat come from?"

"Oh, uh…" She stammered and murmured into his chest before he gently titled her head back to look into her smoke-grey eyes.

"Whass'up?"

"Wellll… I, uhmm." Cidny quickly wilted under Bear's questioning gaze. "Oh, for-get it." She came clean, "Maria mentioned him. But it wasn't really nothing!" She added rather hastily—which caused Bear to bust-out with a deep roaring laugh.

"Ooooooh shit! He gon' tear her lil ass up!"

"Uh-uhnnnn! Bearrrr, stop'itttt." She whined and smacked him across the chest. "She's not like that."

"Oowww! Why you hit me like dat?"

"Oh, I'm sorrr'ryyy." She purred and went to softly rub his chest when he grabbed her and rolled her onto her back. "Heeee!" Cidny eked as she was forcefully pinned; leaving her big round breasts wobbling and swaying beneath Bear's eyes.

"Yo! I told chu before, you too fuckin' heavy handed."

"I said I was sorry." She said in a voice purposely made small and timid—melting Bear's resolve, similar to the way he'd just wilted hers only moments ago.

Bears's body jerked with his sharp intake of breath, as his gaze rose from the large, pink areoles that covered Cidny's mounds. "So, what's up wit'cha girl?"

"I told chuuu. She ain't like that. She's a virgin."

He shrugged, "So what. Cas, will break dat'ass in."

"Quit play'yinnn!" Cidny got mad and twisted away from him. She then sat up against the bed's headboard in a pout.

"What?" He looked up at her with pleading eyes and caressed her inner thigh until she shoved his hand away. "Whass'up, Babe? Tell me."

She shook her head, "I don't wanna go all into her bizness."

Bear laid his huge hand back on her thigh and looked directly into her eyes. "Aye! You s'posed to be my woman, right?

"Uhhh." Cidny's mouth hung slackly open. She knew how she felt, but she wasn't ready for it coming from him. "Ba-Bear." She stuttered.

"Man, I ain't gon' say nuffin."

Cidny launched right into a tale of her and Maria dominating the Wexford young soccer league as 11 year olds. "Even though she was the smallest player in the league, she was faster and stronger than everybody. Even the boys." She went on to tell Bear how she watched from her position guarding the goal, as Maria stole the soccer ball and raced down the center of the field like she'd been shot out of a cannon. "Bear, Maria went to fire one of her Mighty Mouse kicks."

"She do got a mouse nose." He stated, interrupting her tale.

Cidny rolled her big doe-shaped eyes and carried on. "Anywayyyy. She went down right after the kick. And she screamed sooo loud." She wiped at a tear in the corner of her eye. "I can still remember her rolling around in the grass, screaming that she heard something pop between her legs."

"Ouch!" Bear reached for his own groin.

"There was so much blood." She murmured, "I was sooo afraid to get my period after that."

He laid a hand consolingly on her knee as he watched her shake her curly head.

"Later on when we started middle school, she kind of like, changed."

"What'chu mean?"

"She got, like, really mean tempered. I mean it was hard on her; going from being skinny and flat-chested, to having a body like a grown-ass-woman, in one summer's time."

Bear sighed and rolled onto his back, "I guess that's why her crazy'ass be snappin' out at all y'allz games."

"Right." Her head nodded, "And that hot'ass Puerto Rican blood on her mom's side ain't helpin' either."

Offhandedly he said, "Her and my man's would make a helluva combination."

Her chin dropped to her chest and she gave him a look. "Don't start."

"I was just pointin' out that he's half Spanish, too. Mexican." He offered swiftly.

"Oh." She said, forming her mouth into an exaggerated 'O'.

"See, mannn. You all ready to bite my head off."

Cidny's eyes traversed slowly down his body. "I would never bite it off."

A grin expanded across his face, just before she leaned in and bumped him with her shoulder.

"You think Casper would go nuts if he knew that Maria goes commando?"

Bear's eyes got big. "Yo!"

"Yep. And you better not say a word!" She poked him upside the head to emphasize the threat.

"A'ight, but why don't she wear panties?"

"In 10th grade, she got jock itch after wearing sweaty panties home from practice during volleyball season."

Bear entered the little tidbit into his memory bank. "You wanna go out and get somethin' to eat? Maybe see a movie?"

"Okaaaaaay." She said, just as leisurely as her hand slid down past his stomach. "You knooooow." Her hand began to work its magic, "Since I've been spending so much time wit'chuuuu. I really don't get to see her as-."

"Yeah-yeah, we can go get Maria." He said anxiously, and pulled her into a position to straddle him.

Chapter 11

Maria reentered her bedroom with a couple of XXX-movies in one hand and a new underground hip-hop DVD in the other. She'd been picking up the latest dance moves the hip-hop DVD's had to offer since she was a girl—shortly after her mother enrolled her in an African dance class down in the city. She could still recall how amazed the other young girls were when she first revealed that she did not know how to make her booty pop and shake. "Uhm, I know mommy and daddy would rather that I not practice those dances had they seen some of those uncut underground performances." She said, as she thought back on a not so happy time at Ashley's house:

It was the summer before the girls entered the 9th, Maria and Ashley were up in the latter's bedroom, giggling amid the blaring rap music as Maria attempted to teach her very stiff friend how to dance like the Black girls from the hood.

"Hold on, Maria. I need a break." Ashley gasped and reached for the pitcher of strawberry daiquiri, that the resourceful young woman had swiped from her mother's stash.

Meanwhile, unbeknownst to the tipsy pre-teens, Ashley's older brother, Bret, stood in the darkened hallway leering at the sight of Maria's fully developed assets, bouncing enticingly within the confines of her pink bra and panties.

Bret was the Golden Boy. The All-American high school quarterback, who seemed to have it all—any girl he wanted, full ride scholarship to any college in the country. But, he had some very dark, deep-seeded issues.. Try as he might, he could not get the picture of Maria dancing around the room out of his head. *It is almost as if she's dancing for me,* he thought.

Bret left the hall, then, returned a short time later with a couple of fresh daiquiris. "Here Maria, I made this one just for you." He tried not to stare as she naively took the chilled glass that was filled with what they'd already been drinking, plus the crushed half of the date rape pill, GHB...

"Here Maria, lie down and let me get a cool, damp towel." Ashley said as she turned down the music following another half hour of dancing.

"I'm a leeeee'tle light headed." Maria watched a blurry Ashley disappear into her lavish bath, just as Bret entered the room with his shirt off. "Daaaaamn!" She heard herself utter.

No more than five minutes later, Ashley emerged from the bathroom and found her crude brother with his face buried in between the widely gaped thighs of a semiconscious Maria. "Uh-uh don't chu hurt her."

He looked up with a shiny face, "Trust me Ash, she loves every second of this." He dipped in for a few more licks then pulled back to watch Maria squirm and thrust her pelvis. "See, even though she doesn't realize it. She's begging for me. The same way you do."

Ashley knew what her brother was getting ready to do when he stood up and began to unbutton his pants. "No!"

"What?" Bret looked down at his younger sister.

"I'mma tell mom."

He gave her a confident look that meant, *If you tell mom, she's gonna find out about your dirty little secret, too.*

Ashley stood her ground. "Bret, you will get into big trouble if you rape her." She folded her arms after dropping that bomb. "And then you won't get to play with little ole me any longer." She whispered in a tantalizing voice.

Bret left the room after Ashley promised to visit his room before she went to sleep.

"Hey Maria." Ashley eyed her partially nude friend. *I wonder what he put in your drink?* She pondered as she removed her crop top and panties.

"Shhhh." The cunning creature ignored Maria's murmuring protests and proceeded to sample the goodies..

Maria awoke with a start the following morning. She looked at Ashley sound asleep in the bed next to her. Then she groaned as she moved and realized that her panties were glued to her crotch. *Dios Mios (My God)!* Wrongly, she thought she'd thrashed in bed all night in the midst of one of her wild, erotic dreams.

Maria lay there for a moment staring at the ceiling, dwelling and hating her body for something that wasn't even its fault. She could hear her mother now—berating her in an almost playful manner after walking in on her having another sexual dream. *Maria it's because jhu sneak around de' house watching those dirty movies all de' time.* She gently got out of the bed and pulled on her, two sizes too big Rocawear Jeans and a Polo Hoodie that was just as ill-fitting.

Soundlessly leaving the room, Maria took one last glance back at her friend. It was weird, because she vaguely remembered Ashley doing things to her, prior to her doing things to Ashley. *Dios! What is wrong with me?*

Maria took a few shortcuts here and there along with her 30 minute trek through a neighborhood sprawling with magnificent homes; and before she knew it she was standing at the bottom of the long, winding cobblestone driveway that lead up to her happy home. Growing up, Maria's home had always been looked at as the *Hangout Spot* by her and her brother's teammates. Their parents were super- cool and her dad would usually go out of his way to accommodate his children in an effort to make up for the time he'd missed while playing pro football.

That open, happy, loving home could also become a headache for the kids; especially when it came to sleep-overs. Because with their parents being such a highly sexual couple, the muffled noises emitting from their bedroom late at night gave any friend a clear picture of what was underway.

"Euuh!" Maria asserted after cupping a hand over her mouth to cough—her hand and her breath smelt fishy...

Several months after the sleep-over at Ashley's, Maria was two months into her 9th grade year of high school. "Ho'la (Hi)." She greeted a teammate as she strolled down the hallway wearing one of her brother's football jerseys that hung well past her knees. *I can't wait to tell Troy that me and Cid made varsity.*

Suddenly Maria's attention was drawn to the sounds of a big fight going on in the lunch room. When she reached the brawl she was shocked to find her brother fighting with Ashley's brother, Bret. And surprisingly, Bret seemed to be getting the best of Troy.

"Troy! Put jour punches together!" As Maria screamed and shoved her way through the crowd, her brother shook off a hard blow and began to let his hands go—just the way his dad had been teaching him and Maria since they were big enough to punch the heavy bag.

"Uh! Huhh!" Bret took a number of power-packed left hooks to the body, causing him to drop his hands to protect his ribs—leaving his face open. WHA-AAACK! The instant Bret raised his hands to protect his face, Troy sent him crumbling to the floor with another crunching left hook to the ribs. WHA-AAACK!

"Get up! Troy stood over his beaten down quarterback with his huge fists clenched. "I said get up!"

Bret looked up in agonizing pain. "Dude, I think you broke a rib."

"I don't care. Take-back-what chu said about mi lee'tle sister." He demanded, in between labored breaths.

The crowd went silent in anticipation of the revelation, as Bret wiped at his bloody lip and grimaced before speaking. "It's true, man. Just ask her." He pointed in Maria's direction.

It was at that point that Maria wished she could make herself disappear. The news of her and Cidny being named starters for the first time in the school's basketball history seemed irrelevant. She sneered at Bret and thought, *I will never get a guy to date me ahora (now).*

RIIIIINNGGG!

The sound of the phone brought Maria back to present time. "Hellooo."

Cidny was on the line asking her to accompany her and Bear to the movies.

"Nah, uh-uh. I ain't tryin' to be de' third wheel."

"Maria, pu-leeease. You won't be no third wheel. You're supposed to be my gurrrrrl!"

"Yo se (I know). But not today."

After hanging up the phone, Maria glanced down at the two cheerleaders sexually engaged on the DVD's cover. She then pulled the bed sheets over her head.

Chapter 12

"Mariaaaaa!" The shrill of Ms. Toni's high-pitched voice filled the East wing of the mansion.

"What Ma!" She yanked the covers off of her.

"Who de' hell are chu yelling at?" Maria's mother yelled from just down the hall.

Maria quickly changed her tune. "Lo siento Maaaa."

"Si, eso es lo que yo pense (Yeah, that's what I thought)." Ms. Toni said as she shoved open her daughter's door.

Maria's mother was a beautiful, firecracker of a woman that could pass for her older sister. Her high-pitched, nasally voice, along with her New York/Puerto Rican accent, led to her striking resemblance to the Latina actress, Rosie Perez. Ms. Toni had the same thick, full lips as the actress, with a figure that was so curvaceous that the boys up at the high school viewed her as the utmost MILF.

Toni, who was a loving, doting mother, met Maria and Troy's father in college. She was there on a

106

partial volleyball scholarship, and had broken up with her boyfriend back home in Brooklyn, shortly before leaving for school. Toni loved the guy, but he was a bit of a prude. They dated for close to five years without *going all the way.* Until she manipulated him into doing the deed on the night of their senior prom—it was terrible.Toni was unflagging in her zeal to keep trying until they got it right, which never seemed to happen. She stayed with him though, because she did love him. But, when it became painfully evident that he was much more bitter about her leaving than she had initially though, she ended it.

Toni was on her way back to her dorm room in the second of the two towers, the day she met Marty, her future husband: The elevators in Toni's tower were out of service again and she was steaming about having to climb stairs after getting a shower following a particularly irritating practice that saw her volleyball coach ripping her for the slightest mistake. As the libero on her team, Toni understood her responsibility to get the Amazons lined up in the right positions. But being a freshman and standing barely 5'2", 126 pounds, the job was a challenge.

"Vaya (Whew)!" She stopped halfway there to fan her face. She was glad that she happened to be void of the text books in her gym bag today. Toni pinched down the bottoms of her cute, Gap short set and continued up.

Meanwhile, one flight up, Marty Coleman, senior star cornerback and future NFL 1st round draft pick, sat on the cement step, drinking a cold can of beer from the 9-pack that set beside him. He had a date with his two favorite snow bunnies, Mandy and Jessica, as soon as they got out of class and made it up to their dorm room to do what they did best.. Marty was a young man that had his pick of the litter—sexing underclassmen in both towers, the loose girls around campus, and even a few of the sorority girls that thought they were too crafty to fall into the hands of a player such as himself.

Then he spotted one coming up the steps that thus far had eluded him.

Marty crushed the empty can after watching Toni glare at him from the bottom of the stairs for a long silent moment. He knew just who she was. *The Rican chick with the killer body and the stuck-up attitude that played hard to get.* He finally sucked at a tooth and stood up to allow the spicy little Spanish girl in the snug, soft-pink terry cloth outfit, the space to pass.

Toni's nostrils flared in anger after being forced to wait. She hated the way the muscular football player eyed her like a piece of meat from the top step. *Too hood.* She hated his type. She felt that guys like him were nothing more than thugs who got *free rides* because of football. Toni wrinkled her tiny nose as she neared him on the steps. She heard all about the tonto (dumb) coeds that regularly threw themselves at him. "Humph." She huffed, as she tried to avoid him and his strong virile scent on the narrow stairway.

Marty pressed his shoulders to the wall as she went to squeeze by, *Damn! She way hotter than what I imagined.* He thought. *And got damn, she fillin' out them shorts.* He titled his head back and to the side to check out her prominent, bubbled backside. He could not resist.

When his hand palmed her left ass cheek, Toni reacted with a lightning fast smack to the side of his head. "Jhu Mutha-Fuck…" She screeched and kept on swinging.

"Aye! Aye! Ayeee." Marty grabbed hold of her wrists to keep her from hitting him. "Whass wrong wit'chu!" He barked into her face as he spun her around and penned her to the wall with his 5'11", 195 pounds of force. "Calm the-fuck-down."

"Let-Me-Go!" She tried to wrench herself free.

"No!" He yelled back; Which really caused her to snap-out and start to twist and torque her shapely little body while she shrieked and cursed him in Spanish.

"Te odio pendejo! Chinga tu madre! (I hate you! You punk muthafucker!)" Toni's grey eyes were narrowed to angry slits. "Chu fuckin' pato (duck)!

She continued to go on-and-on, spewing threats that Marty could not understand. *Man, this girl is seriously turnin' me the-fuck-on!* He thought to himself as he got a sense that her anger was starting to lessen.

"Whu jhu look at me like dat?" She snarled, then bared her bright white teeth.

"Cause I want kiss you."

Toni's nostrils flared, signaling another tirade when Marty simply went for it and kissed her. "Mmmmmm." And surprisingly, she reciprocated.

She felt Marty's mouth close down on her own in a French kiss that was so hot, it made her utter breathlessly against his lips. "Uhmmm." The feel of his mouth, hot and masculine, assertive—it took her breath away. But then, she became just as aggressive.

The two began to grind against each other, opening their mouths wide, tongue kissing each other passionately—sending eager hands wandering. Marty's hand reached out to squeeze and knead a firmly plumped breast, forcing Toni to whimper something in a language that remained foreign to him. "You smell so good." He muttered as his hot breath teased her ear and neck.

Things were moving too quickly, she was aware of what he was doing, but it felt too good to make him stop. "Nada. Stop. Ooooh, noooo." His steamy, wet lips suckled up to her earlobe. Then his teeth gently bit into and tugged on her ear before tracing it, before dipping inside. "Nuh-uhhhh, uh-uhhhhh."

Slowly, Marty lowered his wet kissing, sucking and nibbling down Toni's neck. He sucked hard enough near the nape of her neck to leave a ring of pleasure when he pulled away to kiss at the bottom of her chin.

Toni gasped in response to him teasingly sucking her top lip into his mouth while her petite hands explored up and down the deeply muscled cut of his back, pulling him into her as her leg curled around him like a smooth beige chicken wing.

Marty's hands fondled each stiff nipple until they extended more than a half of an inch. "Mmmm, I want'chu sooo bad." He growled as a hand slid down inside the back of her shorts to cup one onion- shaped cheek.. A groan issued from deep in his throat when his finger tips brushed the damp, silky hairs between her legs.

"I've never do any t'ing like dis before." She cooed and tucked her face into the crook of his neck. Toni wasn't sure what she wanted as she felt his hands move to encircle her tiny waist to tug her flush

110

with his rigid body, compelling her to feel just how much he wanted her.

They lost all control, leading Marty to roughly yank the crotch of her shorts to the side while she assisted with his sweatpants.

"Ohhhh Gawwwd! Tu asiii grande (It's sooo big)." Toni whimpered out in a strangled sob as the bare head of his penis slipped inside her sopping, gripping sex. "Es muy muchooo."

Marty could not understand that she was trying to tell him that it was too much—her sultry words only spurred him to ease further within her tight, oily nest; until he bottomed-out.

The sound she released was incomprehensible to even someone that fluently spoke Spanish. Marty tried with all his might to stroke slow and easy, but her utterances drove him crazy. "Arghh! Huhhh!" He plunged in and out of her like a piston, pounding her cervix in a way that caused a frantic orgasm to rip through her, simultaneous to the pain..

The sex became fast and furious. Explosive. Supersonic. Toni had straddled his waist with her strong legs, almost as if she were sitting in his lap Indian-style. She moaned and panted while swirling her hips in tune with his ruthless, yet pleasurable thrusts—tightening her legs around his waist.

With her fingers interwined behind his neck, allowing her to lean her shoulder blades back into the wall, Marty was free to plam a bubbly, bouncing cheek in each hand. "Uhhh, yeahhhh."

Suddenly, Toni eked, "Iiieee! Ahi mismo (Right there)! Ahi mismo!! Ahi mismoooo!" She spilled anew, soaking his repeatedly embedding erection with more of her sticky dew. "Dios mios

(Oh, my God). Dios miooos." The mewling cry came as her nails dug into his deep, rich, brown skin.

He pumped her in earnest, his shaft swelling even more within her taut, nipping channel. Then he erupted, ejected, gushing a stream of creamy lava deep inside her core, which heightened her own climax....

Well, eso es todo (that's that). Toni pondered while her body still rippled with the aftershocks as he held her close.

"Th-that was amazing." Marty was bathed in sweat, his muscles beginning to relax. "You a'ight?"

She answered by embarrassingly burying her face into his chest.

"Uhm, uh, I'm sorry." He groaned and laid his cheek against her head.

"Uh-uh, nada. I wanted chu to." She mumbled into his chest.

"Nah." Marty shook his head, "I, uhh, you know."

Toni didn't catch on at first, but when she did she tensed and gulped for air. *Unprotected sex. How stupid can I be?*

Marty effortlessly lifted her to disengage their coupling. Then, as they were rushing to put their clothing into some semblance of order, "Mwah." He leaned in and planted a kiss on her damp forehead.

She smiled sweetly and went back to trying to re-stuff her boob into the cup of her bra. "Para que (What are chu doing)? Toni murmured under her breath.

Man, she's beautiful. He mused while watching her fix her wavy, wet-looking ponytail. "Aye, I'll last longer next time."

Her eyes sparkled as she peered up at him, "Uh, who say dere would be a next time?"

Marty picked up the rest of the beer and headed up the steps behind her. They spent the rest of the day and most of the night, doing things that Toni's unversed young body had only dreamed about.

The following morning Toni awoke glowing, running late for class; and alone. She felt like a fool for a hot second, before coming to the conclusion that he'd given her exactly what she needed. Toni ripped away the sheets that smelt of Marty and their sex. She then took a rushed shower and hurried to class.

While Toni made haste across the grassy courtyard in cutoff frayed jean shorts, flip-flops and a red flannel shirt she wore tied at the bottom to show-off her innie-bellybutton, she spotted Marty. He sat on the benches that bordered the grass, laughing, along with a group of other athletes.

Toni mumbled a curse to herself and continued on her way, *So what if the campus stud scored. I got what I wanted too. Que te parece (How about that)!*

"Hey!" Marty appeared out of nowhere and grabbed her by the elbow. Toni frowned and yanked her arm free.

"Suerta me puneto (Let go of me jhu punk'ass bitch)!" She twisted her arm away with so much force that she almost fell.

"Whoa, whoa." He put up his hands in surrender, as she regained her balance amidst a stream of curses in English and Spanish. "Sorry I rolled out dis morning. But'chu were sleeping so peacefully, and-"

"Save dat shit for one of jour putas! Cause I no need it, Papi."

"Toni, seriously..."

"O'ye!" She cut him off again, but this time it was with an out-thrusted palm.

"Just let me explain." Marty appealed in somewhat of a whine.

"Nada." She squinted up at him as the bright sun rose behind his head, then placed a hand on her hip. "We got busy. And that was that."

"Uh-uh, baby. I'm puttin' my claim down." He glanced back over her shoulder. "That's why all them niggaz is back there laughin'."

Toni used her forearm to block the sun. "Yeah, right." She snorted, a sneer of disbelief, clearly evident in her tone.

"Watch!" He turned toward his boys and point at Toni. "See her. Off the market." With that said, he took her bookbag and began to walk her to class.

"Jhu crazy." She stifled a smile and followed.

"So, uhhhh." He said after only a few steps, "Can I come up and see you after class?"

Now she displayed that lovely, bright smile. "Yo no se (I don't know). Can you?"

Marty gave her a blank stare for a few more paces. "Look, you gon' have to teach a nigga Spanish, so at least I can know when you cussin' me out."

"Ta'bien (Okay)."

He draped an arm over her shoulders as they passed their classmates milling around on the benches. "I don't know what that last word means, but it sounded good."

Si, 'eeet is. 'Eet means okay, or good." She explained.

"Oh, like last night?"

Bashfully, Toni looked down at her toes. "Si. That was muy bien (very good)." She had a brief recollection of just how uninhibited she'd been last night and blushed.

"Hey! Martyyy!" A group of coed's sitting in the grass yelled out in unison.

Toni stopped, shifted her weight sexily to one leg, then gave Marty a sideways look that said, *Uhhh, is jhu gon' check them putas?*

He flashed that arrogant grin that was the source of many young women around campus creaming their panties. "C'mere." He dropped Toni's bookbag and encircled her tiny waist with his hands, "Gimme a kiss."

"Ooooooh!" The coed's all howled—some more jealous than others, as they watched the hunky athlete kiss the Spanish girl.

Toni and Marty became inseparable on the Oakland campus. Toni even hooked her only friend on the volleyball team at the time, Trisha, with Mike, a 6'6", 310 pound white lineman that roomed with Marty. Then, approximately 9 months later; Toni made her debut on all of the big sports networks when she went into labor on National Television, just as Marty was selected with the 4th pick of the NFL draft by the Miami Dolphins.

Chapter 13

Ms. Toni stood just inside Maria's doorway eyeing the various trophies, awards and academic achievements that covered her child's walls. "Jhu really need to, basta ya (cut it out). With all of dis moody meirda (shit). Chu too old for it."

Maria sat there with her pug nose wrinkled, waiting for her mother to tell her why she'd busted into her room.

"Oh." She said all willy-nilly, as she picked up the DVD with the naughty cheerleaders on the cover and tucked it into the pocket of her silk kimono. "Jhu got some guests waiting for jhu downstairs."

Maria went lazily down the stairs ahead of her mother, then rolled her eyes at the sight of Cidny and Bear sitting on the couch. "What are j'all doing here?" She asked with a pout.

"Mariaaaa!" Her mother screeched on the stairs behind her. "Dat is no way jhu greet. Dejar de actin' like chu are spoiled."

"Maaaaa."

"Don't Maaa, me. Dese guys were nice enough to invite chu to de' movies."

"Maaaa, Yo no (I don't)-"

Ms. Toni cut her off. "Jhu go up and get dressed. Because jhu going."

"It's okay, Ms. Toni." Cidny intervened. "She don't gotta-"

"Nada!" Toni silenced her, but added a genuine smile. "She goin', cause me and Mr. Coleman want de' casa to ourselves, esta noche (tonight)."

"Ohhhh, okaaaay." Cidny smiled just as sweetly.

Maria mumbled past her mother on her way back up the stairs. "J'all didn't have enough fun earlier?"

"I guess not." Toni replied sarcastically and tapped the plastic DVD case sticking out of her pocket. "I t'ink we gon' watch a movie."

"Euuuuuh!" She shrieked as she ran upstairs to get dressed.

In the weeks following that night out at the movies with Cidny and Bear, Maria would go on to hang-out with the young couple from time-to-time at Bear's house. The girls even got *glammed-up* a time or two to hit the club scene with Bear....

"Nah, no offense Bear." Maria said as her and Cidny sat in his living room chopping it up. "I'm sure jour boy Casper is cool and allll."

"I'm sayin' doe," Bear leaned forward in his seat. "you ain't really got to know him."

"Mieda (Look), I ain't de' una (one)." Her neck snaked and twisted to assert the point. "He's

117

not gon' be adding me to de' lista of putas he slayed. Ya heard!"

Maria pushed a lock of dark wavy hair behind her ear and took a sip of beer from the bottle. The majority of her cousins up top, in the Bushwick section of Brooklyn, were Latin Kings. So she knew all about *street dudes* and how that part of the game went down. Fast money. Fast women.

There was noooo doubt in Maria's mind that Casper was the last thing she needed. She had strong self-esteem, which would never allow her to be the type of girl who let herself get used and run-over by a guy, just because he was *that somebody*.

Bear continued to press the issue on his boy's behalf. "See, like I was tellin' Cid... You and Casper are too much alike. That's why y'all stay at each other's throat."

With a flick of her wrist, Maria flea'd him, "Pu-leeeease."

"Yeahhh, Mariaaa." Cidny jumped in with a whiney plea. "I think y'all would be cute together."

"Cute!" She frowned her face up like she'd just sucked on a bitter lemon instead of a Budweiser bottle.

"What?" Cidny questioned, wide-eyed.

"I ain't no fuckin' puppy." She sneered evilly.

"See! That's what I'm talkin' 'bout." Bear jabbed a finger toward Maria. "My man Casper will take care of that slick mouth, and evil attitude."

"Psshhhh! He ain't takin' care of nu'ting ova' here." Maria humphed. Her future was too bright. She was starting college soon, and there was nothing that a no good drug dealer that fucked anything with a cute face, could do for her.

Chapter 14

After nearly two months of the small Midwestern town in Kansas, Casper was bored and kind of homesick. The novelty of helping out at his uncle's construction business had lost its luster. Currently, Casper sat on the couch inside his Uncle Harold's modest three bedroom home reading "Dawn of the Empire", a novel by Sam Barone. It was a story about a superior thinker/strategist, who overcame the odds and built the first walled city.

Once he finished the book he went back to the beginning to read Fly's quote one more time, *'Those in positions of power need to stay two to three moves ahead of those that are envious'*.

Casper sighed and stared at the wall. He thought about heading over to the site. The first time he set foot on his Uncle's work site.. it was in the opening stages; flattened dirt and clay with bright orange flags flying from wooden stakes sticking out of the ground, where future foundations would set to support office buildings. And off to the far left was the big white trailer with the Port-o-Potty beside it;

which was where his Uncle's partner's daughter took care of the paperwork and other Administrative duties.

The first day that Casper saw Misty working in the trailer, he thought, *Hey, she ain't bad lookin'; and she holdin'.* She reminded him of the American Idol singer, Kelly Clarkson, but with a head of curly red hair that she wore in a pixie-cut:

"Hi, Mr. Smith." Misty greeted Casper's Uncle that first day in the trailer.

"I told you to call me, Harold." He grumbled. "That shit makes me feel old."

"Oh sorry, Harold." Her lashes batted sweetly, prior to her gaze falling on Casper who laid-back by the door. "Soooo, this must be your nephew."

"Nice to meet chu." Casper said as his dark eyes dropped to her overly exposed cleavage.

"Same here." Her enticing twins threatened to spill out, as she leaned over the desk to shake Casper's hand. "I, oh!" Misty jerked backwards the instant, a showboating Master rose up on his hind legs and slapped his paws atop her desk.

"Boah!" Harold barked. "I told chu to leave dat damn hound at the house."

"Ooohhh!" She squealed and patted the top of Master's head. "He's sooo cute. And I just love his cat eyes."

Harold groused about the dog being on site until he left out the trailer.

The moment the trailer door closed, Misty was out of her seat and strutting toward the file cabinet. "I don't know why your Uncle would say that your dog's a violation on site. It's totally untrue."

Casper barely heard a word as he checked out the way her thick little figure filled out the tie-dyed, Guess, ankle skinny jeans. *Damn she got a nice ass; white girl or not.*

"So, uhh, where ya from?" She asked over her shoulder, with a slight country drawl.

"Oh, uh. I'm from all over the Northeast."

Her stare was measured. "Yeahhh, you remind me of those laid-back L.A. guys that I ran into when I went to UCLA."

"What made you leave there, to come back here?"

"I love my home town." Misty eked in a girlish tone as she laid a hand on his forearm.

"I ain't mean it like that. But, uhhh, what do y'all do out here?"

Her eyes seemed to twinkle, "Besides lots of sex. I teach a yoga class."

Casper did not miss the hint, or her body language. "Yoga, huh?"

"Yep, I'm pretty good." Misty slowly licked her lips. "I like the Adho Mukha Svanasana pose."

"Oh." His head nodded. "Downward facing dog."

"You know your stuff."

A cocky grin came to the corner of his mouth. "I know some things."

"I bet'chu do." She eyed him hard. "I would love for you to come by one of my classes."

He looked around and shook his head, "I don't know about all dat."

"I can arrange a private class, if you'd like?"

Chapter 15

A month or so after that initial meeting with Misty, Casper was in a large field down the street from the work site with Master. "Arff! Harfff!" The dog barked wildly.

He threw the handball as far as he could, "Go get it, boy!"

The dog's powerful paws dug into the turf, propelling him across the field like a rocket. Casper watched Master fly as he thought about the things Misty did last night. The girl was an amazing nympho. She had definitely opened his eyes when it came to sexual experimentation.

Then he began to think about Bear and what he'd learned from their, secret, weekly phone calls. Bear had fallen very hard for Cidny, which made Casper worry even more about one of their enemies trying to kill Bear while he was O.T. (out of town). "Nah, I'm sure that Nigga can take care of his self." He started to think about the time he and Bear tried to run up on a guy named Rock, and he laughed as he threw the ball again.

They were riding in a rented Lincoln Town Car with Fly when Bear spotted the dude who had shot Fly. "Yo! Dere go Rock, right dere."

Rock was pulled up at the curb talking to two girls that went to school with Casper and Bear, so he never noticed them ride past in the Lincoln.

Fly wanted to put the work in himself, but his lungs were still healing from the three slugs he'd taken in the back. So he reluctantly let Casper and Bear out of the car. "I'll pick y'all up over on Thomson Street."

Casper and Bear jogged down a side street and came around the building, just as Rock pulled off. "Shit!" They ran back the way they'd come and caught up to him as he made the right turn. BOOM! BOOM! BOC! BOC! BOC! BA-BOC! BOOM! BOOM!

Standing side-by-side, Casper fired a Glock while Bear unloaded with a 44. The rounds blew out the windshield and Swiss cheesed the side of the car. But somehow, Rock yanked the wheel hard to the left and peeled out on them—leaving them in the smoke of his burnt tires. Then to make matters worse, Fly laughed despite the pain of punctured lungs, to the point that he had to go back into the hospital for a few days...

Casper looked toward the woods bordering the field and had to laugh himself, because the day Fly got out the hospital, he took him and Bear out to his friend Sparky's shooting range; out in the country, where the little old redneck drilled them on their shooting skills for days. "Master."

In mid-sprint, the pit bull slid to a stop with the handball in his slobbery mouth and stared at a rabbit watching him from the trees.

"Skit'em boy!" He sent the dog into attack mode.

Casper attempted to follow Master through the trees and brush as he darted here and there in pursuit of the furry little creature. He jumped over downed trees, over and through sticking bushes—lost Master, then caught sight of him before running through some denser underbrush that brought him around a big hill and a giant truck-sized boulder—running himself smack into Master, squaring off with an overgrown wild pig.

The boar was well over 300 pounds and very aggressive. It shuffled to the right, and then to the left, it's long yellowish white tusks snapping the entire time. CLA-AAACK! CAA-LAACKKK!

"No! Master, come here!" Casper yelled, which drew the attention of the boar. The spiked fur covering its thick neck and shoulders appeared to ripple as white, stinking foam bubbled from its mouth.

The boar's beady red eyes zeroed in on Casper, milli-seconds before it charged and knocked him off his feet.

"Umphh!" He hit the ground and looked up as the animal circled, just as he tried to scamper to his feet. "Oh, shiiiit!"

Casper was slow in his effort to roll away, but Master jumped onto the wild boar's back before he could sink his razor sharp teeth into Casper's leg. "Aarrr!" It screeched and bucked, while swinging its powerful head in a bid to either gore Master, or shake him loose..

The pit bull is a breed of dog that was bred for this particular type of combat, which allowed Master to use his superior intelligence and instincts to pivot easily away from the boar's charges and tusk stabs. He then darted in—narrowly avoiding a slicing tusk, to sink his jaws deep within the animal's thick hide. It shrieked and rolled its massive body through the nearby brush; thus, goring and throwing Master free.

The dog never even yelped in pain as the two came to their feet in a small clearing.

"Look out, Master!" Casper yelled as he missed the boar's face with a nice sized rock. "Ahhh! Ah!" He smacked that animal as hard as he possible could with a rusted pipe, and it hardly looked his way.

The boar wanted Master so bad that it could taste it. It had a set of shredded ears, old cuts and scratches, even a broken tusk—all of which testified to the battles it fought to secure the sows to bear its offspring.

Master, with his shoulder wound leaking blood, wasted little time in resuming the attack. He darted in, then out—tricking the boar into a wrong move that gave him a tattered ear to grab a hold of. Next, as the beast drove him backwards, he used its own momentum as he twisted away, to wrestle it to the ground. It squealed and squirmed wildly, kicking its stubby legs while its face was penned in the dirt.

As Casper looked around for a sharp rock to bash the wild boar's head in, he saw that the animal had begun to really foam at the mouth and snort so hard that puffs of dirt blew into the air. *Master is usin' his smarts to tire out this fuckin' monster.* All at once, time stopped as the boar swung it's head and slashed Master. "Mutha Fuckerrrr!" He ran over and kicked it in the face a few times before it got to its feet.

Master icily looked up toward Casper—he'd maintained the hold on the boar's ear the entire time. He appeared to smile with those green eyes, just before releasing a growl and torquing his head to violently rip what remained of the animal's ear from its head. "Hiiieeee!" It squeaked.

"Harrrrrrr." A low growl rumbled from Master's throat as he circled the boar with the bloody ear in his mouth, like, *You want this? Come and get it.*

This boar snarled, made a weak charge that Master easily dodged, sending it right on by—right into Casper.

"Uuhhhh!" The beast slammed into him with all of its force. Then as it frantically tried to gore Casper, its tusk got snagged on the leg of his baggy jeans and it began to drag him across the rocky dirt on his stomach.

"Keeeeee!" Suddenly the boar released a loud, ear-splitting screech.

Casper ripped his pants leg free of the tusk and rolled onto his side to see that Master had jumped on the pig's enormous hairy back, where he managed to lock on at the base of the animal's neck. The muscles in the pit bull's jaws and shoulders bulged as his teeth dug in with nearly three thousand pounds of bite pressure per square inch, to tug and yank until he ripped out a portion of bloody spine and brain stem.

The boar collapsed in a heap, plunging the wooded area into silence. Master walked around the dead animal and sniffed a few times before shaking his head to get the stench out of his nose. He then limped over to Casper and they headed back the way they'd come.. The pit bull was more than resilient, but as they got near the field the blood was pumping from his shoulder.

Casper picked up his dog and carried him through the cluster of trees, out across the field and onto the shoulder of the highway to hike back to the work site.. As Casper hustled down the road with the bloodied pit bull cradled in his arms and motorists gawking at the sight, he began to try to gauge how badly Master had been injured when a horn blew behind him.   HONNNNK! HOONNNNNK!

"Yo!" He turned and nearly went down.

Misty stuck her red head out of her Subaru, "What happened?" She cried out.

"Let's go. He needs a vet." Casper told her as he got into the backseat with Master across his lap.

Misty took them to a veterinarian that usually attends her yoga classes, where the woman promptly treated and cleaned the wounds while her brother, the local game warden, went back with Casper and his partner to test and dispose of the dead boar...

"Awwlll, he's sooo brave and strong." Misty and the vet chorused, near tears as they all sat around with the game wardens, listening to Casper retell the epic battle between the wild boar and Master.

Once the tests came back negative for rabies, Casper said his goodbyes and scooped up Master.. "What?" He looked at Misty, gloating from behind the wheel.

"Nothingggg. I was just." She eyed him shyly and tucked in her bottom lip. "It's a good thing you caused me to come to work late this morning, huh?"

His brow came together, "What'chu mean?"

Alabaster skin from her cleavage to her cheeks turned a rosy red.. Last night, Misty had sucked Casper until he was harder than re-enforced steel. She then used her soft hands to apply a special lubricant to his stiff shaft, prior to introducing him to the pleasures of anal sex. "I think we both know that you enjoyed my treat, a little too much."

He licked at his lips and tried not to grin in response, "Oh that?"

"Yes, thaaat." Demurely, Misty looked away and savored an intimate tenderness between her bottom cheeks.

Chapter 16

Harold pulled up in front of his house and spotted his partner's daughter, Misty, leaving out the front door with a big smile on her face. *She certainly looks like she got everything she came to get.*

"Misty!" The shout stopped her in her tracks.

She turned, "Oh, hi, Mr. Ha-   I mean, hi Harold."

Following a brief conversation about the work site payroll, Harold watched Misty saunter over to her car. *When the hell did they start makin' white girls with rear-ends like that?* He pondered as he entered the house through the kitchen. He frowned at Master staring at him from his spot curled up on the floor, then hugged his wife.

"Harold." Hilda said in a whisper, before looking around as if someone might hear her.

"Woman, say what'chu gon' say in your own kitchen. You ain't gotta whisper."

The full-figured beauty placed both hands on her hips and glowered at her husband until he finished. "Uh, who you think you talkin' to?"

He stammered out a quick concession while she waved him quiet with a flick of her dish towel.

"I came home from grocery shopping and… Mm-mmm! That lil white girl was up there carryin' on like Reece was killin' her."

Yep! That boah a showw-nuff Smith. He had himself a good chuckle as he listened to his wife go on with the story…

"Reece." Harold sat down on the couch with Casper to have an old-fashioned, man-to-man. "I love you too death, boah. But don't put me in no sticky situation with my business partner."

"I ain't Unk. I got'chu."

"Naw!" He shook his head and scratched at his graying beard. "God forbid that girl come up pregnant or catch serious feelings for your narrow ass."

"I got it under control. She's…"

"Just don't put me in no bind. Shit! That girl pop out a black baby," He eyeballed Casper. "I'mma have to bury her old man."

Master limped into the living room to see what all of the laughing was about.

"Right on time!" Casper said amidst the laughter.

The pitbull stared at him for a pause, then, lapped his pink tongue back inside his mouth. Master did not enjoy the medicine—especially when it was time for the two pills to be inserted into his rectum.. "Harrfff!" He released a sharp bark in protest and limped back into the kitchen.

* * *

Later on that evening, Casper called Bear on a prepaid phone. "'Sup man? What's good out dere?"

Bear began to talk about a few random events, before he let Casper know in a coded message, that the police were not actively seeking him in regards to Court and Rabbit's murder.

"So, uhh, whass up wit'chu and Cid? Y'all still doin' y'all?"

Bear glanced over at Cidny who was curled up on the couch beside him, "We good. Somebody side-swiped her pop's truck the other day. So, I had it towed to the shop and handled that."

"Ahaaa!" He laughed on the other end, "She got'chu open like dat? You all in the family, huh?"

"Chillll, Cuuuzzzz." His deep voice rumbled.

"Puppy love'ass nigga." Casper teased.

He chuckled and cut his eye to make sure Cidny was watching the movie. "Real talk... She an animal."

"Bearrr!" She smacked his thigh. "Why you tell him thaaaat?"

"C'mere." He draped an arm around her shoulders and pulled her close to him. But she drew herself away from him and pouted.

As Casper listened to Bear sweet-talk Cidny through the phone, a picture of Maria popped into his head—pouty little mouth, green eyes, the light dusting of freckles sprinkled across the bridge of her tiny mouse-like nose, that cute raspy Latina accent of hers; and that ignorant snobbish attitude. *I can't stand that bougie-ass bitch. She think she better than a nigga 'cause she come from the suburbs.* Casper could not understand why Bear wanted to get wifed-up with a girl that he didn't even know.

131

"Yo!" Bear husked when he finally got back on the phone.

"Damn nigga. You act like I ain't callin' long-distance."

"My bad, homie. But look, I'mma get'chu plugged wit' Maria, as soon-"

"I'm already on my way back. And yo, all I'mma do is fuck da bullshit outta that lil' stuck-up bitch."

"I can't wait for you to get back, man. And as far as the little Mamacita go, for real." He shrugged on the other end, "I kicked it with her and Cid a few times. She's an official thoroughbred."

Casper chuckled, "C'mon man."

"Watch." He said, in total confidence. "I ain't even gon' say that I told chu so."

* * *

Grieve, Smoke and Ralphy sat on the concrete benches out in front of the Trackstone housing project highrise watching the booming, hand-to-hand drug sales they now controlled, thanks to Smoke's older brother.

"Homiez!" Grieve ranted as he inhaled the smoke from his Newport, "I know dat nigga Casper did my bro."

Ralphy nodded in agreement and added, "All of a sudden he s'posed to be O.T. (out of town)."

"Yeah, that ain't no fuckin' conincidence." Smoke offered.

The three young men were born and raised in this particular project; and all of them had been putting in work since the minute they were able to pick-up a gun and steal a car.

Smoke flicked a burning butt at the feet of a man walking by, "My man said he seen Bear the otha' day, down the new club."

"Which one?" Grieve was all ears.

"Club Aqua." He replied as the man smartly kept walking.

His jaw clenched as a dark-skinned girl with a very big booty strolled by. "Yo! Hold up." Grieve shouted at the girl before turning back to the others, "Y'all gon' make sure the word get out about the bread we got on them niggaz?"

"We got'chu." Smoke spoke for himself and his homie. Now that his brother, Big Crusher, was supplying them with large quantities of drugs, they had the ability to throw their weight around and put lucrative contracts out on Bear and Casper's lives.

"A'ight then, y'all. I'mma go holla at this shawty real quick."

Ralphy and Smoke watched as Grieve caught up to the girl, then went with her around to the back of the highrise, where they knew the two would sniff a bag of dope—prior to a round of sex on the stairwell.

"Why don't the nigga just take da' hoe up to one of the apartments?" Smoke said, aloud, more to himself than his homie.

"Fuck all dat! What that nigga need to do, is stop blowin' all that heroin."

Smoke looked at Ralphy, "Right! You need to check him..."

In turn, Ralphy gave him a look that said, *Yeah, right!*

Chapter 17

By the end of the week, Casper was back home. The first thing he took care of was Master's doggy door. "Boy, I gotta lock you in the loft so you don't go out there and run around down by the river."

Master gave a short whining sound, the way he would when he really wanted something.

"No, man. I'm not gon' be tryin' to give you baths with those stitches. And you better not bust 'em open while I'm gone." He mixed up a bowl of Eukanuba dog food with a can of gourmet dog food, gave Master a fresh bowl of water, then headed over to Bear's house to surprise him…

"Hey!" Cidny greeted Casper at the door with a big hug.

Damn, she done changed. Casper thought as Cidny yelled up to Bear and lead the way into the living room where she continued to dust while she talked to him. He could not believe the transformation that had taken place with her in barely two months time. Her naturally curly hair was pressed and styled like she'd been to one of the hood's hair salons.

"You just got back this afternoon, right?"

"Yeahhhh. I would have been back earlier, but I wanted to get my dog checked out by the vet one last time before I rolled."

"Yeah, Bear told me about that guy. He's sooo brave and smart." She added.

He agreed and observed as she stretched her barefoot, 6'2" shapely frame to dust the top of the mantel. *Whoa!* Casper looked away when she began to dust the lower portion of the fireplace and the tops of her heavy breasts wobbled inside the bra she wore beneath her midriff-baring cutoff wifebeater.

"Lil nigga!" Bear barked as he came down the stairs with a huge smile on his face.

Casper did not miss the intense double-take his homie took of the bright orange, skintight, fleece short-shorts that Cidny's pliant flesh filled out so well. "'Sup, big head." He gave Bear a knowing grin.

Bear scratched at his nappy beard and sat down as Cidny left the room to the sounds of Jadakiss bumping from the speakers, *Why Halle have to let a cracka' pop her to get an Oscar... Why?* He started to tell Casper about his run-in with a Trackstone Crip:

Bear went down to Walker's Sneaker Spot to buy a new pair of Air Force Ones, and while in the midst of browsing, a short chubby dude bumped by him, then gave him a "mad dog" stare.

"You should have knew what was up when he gritted on your big ass." Casper offered.

"Right." He replied, with a shrug of his thick shoulders, "And I knew he was left lanin' from the gate with all da' blue he had on. So I gave him a pass, but then I catch him given me grimy looks later on. I'm like, Yo! This fool gotta be strapped."

Bear then explained to Casper how he slipped out of the store and allowed the guy to assume that he was unarmed and trying to make it to his car for a weapon.

But, that actually wasn't the case!

As Bear sold the game to the fullest by fast-walking and cutting down a side street, the overconfident Crip ran up on him with his handgun concealed behind his thigh.

"'Sup Nigga!" The guy wolfed recklessly—feeling as though he were about to put down a notorious, Wilson Works Crip. "You know what da' fuck it-"

BOC! BOC! Bear spun and cut the Westsider off in the middle of his statement—hitting him twice, before he could even raise his cannon. The first two shots from the small caliber handgun struck the young man in the face and neck and spun him halfway around before he fell to the ground in between two parked cars.

With horns blaring from the congested traffic on nearby Broad Street, no one seemed to hear the gunshots or notice the dead body, as Bear swiftly made his exit from the murder scene..

"How you know he was from da' Trackstone?" Casper asked as Cidny came bouncing into the room with beers for everyone.

"Cause the city was talkin' 'bout that shit."

After setting the beers down on the black coffee table, Cidny stood wide-legged in front of Bear and dropped her chin to her chest while she retied the

136

drawstring to her shorts, "Talkin' about what?" She asked without actually thinking about the question.

"Babe." Bear said tenderly.

"Oh, I'm sorry." She replied just as tenderly, and plopped her warm pillow-like buns down sideways on his lap.

It was more than a struggle for Casper not to gawk at the way her knockers strained against her bra strap, so he broke the ice. "Yo Cid! You do know that chu workin' wit' a lil too much to be runnin' around in them tiny-ass shorts, right?"

She pursed and twisted her full, thick lips prior to offering a retort. "Maria fills hers out the same way."

Casper watched her gently smooth the hair down the side of her head. "Where did dat come from?"

Cidny simply smacked her lips and smiled in response.

Following twenty minutes of drinking beer and laughing, Cidny got up off of Bear's lap to look back behind herself as she pinched down the shorts in his face.

"Where you goin'?" He eyed her tugging at her bottoms to keep them from riding up over her rounded humps of her smooth cakes.

"I gotta pee." She whispered. "Dag, gone in 60 seconds."

"What'chu say?" Bear growled.

"Nothing." Cidny said sweetly on her way out the room.

Cidny issued the "60 seconds" comment due to a wrestling match in the kitchen a few days ago, that lead to a quickie, in which Bear ejaculated prematurely in only a handful of strokes...

Sometime later, Cidny reentered the living room while tying a silk wrap around her head to keep her hairstyle in proper order. Then, she smiled at Casper and smirked at Bear, as an unaware Maria stepped into the room behind her.

"Uhhh!" Maria's mouth froze in a silent 'O' before her cute face transformed into an evil snarl. "Para que!" She turned on Cidny and sparked off in anger. "Para que? No te de verguenze?"

Rapidly, Maria questioned why Cidny would set her up in such a way; As Cidny argued her point, in Espanol, just as hasty.

"Aye!" Bear barked at Cidny, "I asked you not to talk dat Spanish shit wit' me in da' room."

Cidny frowned and tucked in her bottom lip like a school girl who had just been scolded by her teacher. "Lo siento, Papi."

"Shit. I don't like dat shit. I don't like not knowin' what people sayin' around me." He grumbled under his breath while Casper looked down at a scuff on the side of his halfway laced butter Timberland boots. "Sorry, is the only word I know. Shit."

Maria huffed, "Pshhh!" She did not give a fuck about Bear's issue. *I can't believe dis puta just backdoored me.*

Cidny was preparing to say something, "Maria..." when she was silenced by the universal stop sign.

"Me importa un pito (I couldn't care less)." Maria grumbled as she removed her coat.

Casper huffed and grumbled to himself, when he looked up and saw that customary evil glare on Maria's face. *I'm outta here.* He thought. But, right before he was about to get up off the couch, Maria unclenched her jaw, sat down next to him and flashed a smile that lit up the room.

"Hola (Hi)." She softly bit into her bottom lip and waited for his reaction.

Casper sat there stunned as Cidny and Bear looked on like two proud matchmakers, before quickly realizing what they were doing.

"Uh Bear, let me talk to you." Cidny led the way out of the room.

"'Sup." Casper rubbed at his cheek and slyly checked out Maria's knockers for the first time. Today, instead of her usual hoodie or sweat shirt; she'd worn a tight long john shirt under a tan t-shirt, which hugged her just enough to show the true size and shape of her prominent grapefruits.

"I didn't know chu were back."

"Yeahhh, I just got in."

"Hmmmm." She hummed softly and allowed her eyes to roam the room. *I don't know what to say. What do I say?* She pondered nervously. *I am sooo glad I washed my hair today. Dios Mios! Do mi breath smell?* There were so many thoughts bouncing around in her head as she sat beside Casper—knees gaped wide, like a dude.

Casper peeped the way Maria dug her fingers into her knees, to the point that her knuckles were white. "Aye, uhmmm, you want a beer?"

"Uh-hmmm." Her head nodded so vigorously that her wavy ponytail flopped around.

"Cid! Grab Maria a brew."

She bit at the inside of her mouth to keep from smiling too hard. "I thought jhu was going to get it."

He shrugged, "We guests."

"Right." Maria exaggeratedly rolled her green eyes.

With the ice now broken, they all sat around the living room drinking beer, talking and listening to music—when Cidny abruptly turned down the stereo and asked Casper to tell Maria about how his pit bull fought off a wild boar..

"Awwww!" Maria and Cidny cooed softly, following the story.

"A'ight-a'ight!" Bear wrinkled his face, "Cid, grab dat jar of Pineapple Kush from da' spot upstairs."

"Okay." She popped up, pinched down the material of her shorts riding up her thighs and went to get the weed.

The four of them sat around; smoked, laughed, and then smoked some more.

"Aaaahhh! That was my jam!" Cidny came out of her weed-smoke induced lull to bob her head to Salt-N-Pepa's late 80's hit. "Yeeeeah... Shaahhh! Push it. Push it reeeal good!"

Bear stretched as the room appeared to perk up.

"C'mon y'allll!" Cidny chirped. "Let's go out and do somethin'."

"I'm hungry." Maria mumbled, followed by 'me too' from Bear and Casper; which put a slight damper on Cidny's partying plan.

"Well, I ain't cookin'." She said in a pout.

Bear gave Maria a sideways look, *I don't have a problem with that.*

Cidny caught Bear making fun of her cooking skills and shoved him upside the head. "Don't play." Her grey eyes narrowed evilly to establish that point. "Anyway. We can go out to eat."

Maria took one look down at her oversized, slashed and frayed biker jeans and shook her head. She did not want to go out to a place where the females would be dressed and glammed, while she looked like a little dike-biker reject. "Uh-uhnnn, I ain't goin' to no clubs lookin' like this."

Casper leaned in and playfully bumped shoulders with her, "You look al'ight to me."

Maria could not hide the way the breath exited her lungs, nor could she hide the way her cheeks and ears began to glow a deep red. "Gracias, gracias." Her nervous, always scratchy voice rasped.

I can't wait to hear the hoarse raspy noises she gon' make when I get her knees pushed back by her ears. Casper thought, as he watched Maria overbite her bottom lip and lean forward to hear what Cidny was saying over the music.

Cidny used the remote to turn down the stereo, "I said we can go out to Dave & Buster's, get somethin' to eat and play some games."

"I'm wit' dat." Bear said, followed by Casper.

"I'mma get dressed."

Bear eyeballed the way Cidny's rear bounced and quivered, as she bounded out of the room and up the stairs. "I gotta get dressed too."

Chapter 18

Casper and Maria sat together on the couch enjoying each other's company as the conversation flowed easily between them. Every now and then, she would lightly touch his arm or knee to emphasize a point like; how good she played basketball and how she would beat him in a game of one-on-one.

"Lil lady, I don't know about all dat." He scratched at his shadowed down facial hair and stared into her eyes until she was forced to bashfully look down at her hands folded in her lap.

"Man, they sure been up dere for a while." She said as she averted his dark brown eyes.

"Hmmm." Casper continued to watch as she adorably refused to meet his gaze. "I'm gettin' ready to say fuck them, and sneak up outta here wit'chu."

Her eyes remained demurely riveted on her lap, "Ohh."

This was the first time in Maria's life that she'd been left alone with an aggressive, young Black male from the inner city. As a result, she had zero experience when it came to dealing with the situation she presently found herself in. Where she came from, the boys were well-mannered most of the time, rich, and always afraid of her Hulk-sized big brother.

Maria could feel Casper's eyes intently watching her, as her eyes looked anywhere but into his. "They probably up there doin' it." She blurted before she got a chance to pull the thought back inside of her mouth. *Did I just say that? Tonto (Dummy)!*

Casper found Maria's nervousness cute and innocent. So he allowed the pause to go on for a few more seconds. "Aye." He tapped her knee with the back of his hand. "Haaa, dey up dere like rabbits." He said with a chuckle.

"Ahaaa. Yep." Instantly, Maria was at ease as she leaned into Casper and giggled while he chuckled until Cidny came down the stairs.

"What ch'all laughin' about?" Cidny asked as she finished slipping on a short-cut leather blazer, paired with a pair of tight wine-colored Armani Exchange jeans.

"Nothin'!" They replied simultaneously, which caused them to look at each other and burst into even more raucous laughter.

Cidny shook her head, waved her hand and went into the kitchen.

Maria looked up from a moment of her and Casper's kush-weed induced laughing and saw Bear staring at them from the stairs. To her, he looked very mature in the expensive, brown Canali turtleneck that she watched Cidny spend nearly half of her savings on.

"I see y'all getting' along." Bear offered in that slow, deep drawl of his.

Maria stifled a giggle and brought her mouth close to Casper's ear. "He sounds like Yogi de' Bear."

"Aaaaaah!" They both howled...

Once the group of four arrived at the Southside Dave & Buster's in Bear's truck, Casper and Maria headed straight for the Elite Ops military operations game located on the center floor of the establishment.

"Go left! Go left! Jhu otha' left!" Maria directed Casper as they teamed-up to advance swiftly through the complicated stages of a game which consisted mainly of shooting and blowing up the enemy by any means necessary.

"See dat shit!" He remarked out of the side of his mouth as he put down a sniper that had a bead on Maria. "I got'chu."

Maria's emerald green eyes blazed for a split-second, as she deftly gave Casper a sideways glance. Then she cleverly dialed up a bazooka and used its armor-piercing rocket to destroy a tank that was about to rundown her overconfident partner. "Jhu welcome." She taunted.

He nodded his head and continued to fire on threats that arose from behind partially collapsed walls, blown out buildings, and even the occasional still burning vehicle. "I love da' way you talk wit' dat lil Rican accent."

She twisted her little mouth and saved Casper from another sniper, "Lo que'sea."

Casper took the proper precautions for any other future sniper.. "What do dat word mean?"

"It means, what'eva." Maria explained, as she moved her fighter in front of Casper's to take the lead.

"I had-"

"Shhhh!" She shushed him…

Later on when the food came, Casper grabbed at the crotch of his crisp dark-colored Orisue jeans, to adjust his package as he sat down in the booth with Maria, Bear and Cidny, to dig into a table full of Buffalo wings, deep-fried shrimp, steak salads and fries.

"Uhh, guys, I'mma need to see ID's." The waiter asked when he sat down two huge pitchers of beer—leading the entire group to pull out the fake ones they own.

Casper was seriously feeling Maria's tomboyish style, even though she daintily held the Buffalo wing with the tips of her fingers, like she was afraid to get sauce on her hands as her teeth ripped the meat from the bone. "Girl, you can put down some food to be so small."

Maria cupped a hand over her partially full mouth and nodded in agreement while speaking to Cidny in Spanish.

"Yo Cid, what I tell you 'bout dat?" Bear grumbled.

She ignored him, rolled her grey eyes and clucked her tongue. "Mine's too, Jelly. Mine's too."

Casper was silent for a moment before calculatingly turning his gaze on Cidny. "Now I know how Bear feels."

"Awww." Cidny puckered her lips and purred to him as if he were a cute puppy; then, she began to speak without giving her brain a chance to tell her not to, "Maria was just saying that everything she eats goes to her bu…" Her eyes suddenly widened, after she got kicked under the table.

"Maldito (Damn'it)! If I wanted the'eeeem to know that, I would have said it in English." Maria articulated with a hot, twist and roll of her neck.

Meanwhile, Casper sat nearby, unknowingly allowing himself to be drawn to and fascinated by— Maria's feisty personality and unique mixture of tomboyish-sexiness. He sucked at his teeth and tilted his head to indicate what was behind her, "Jelly? That's what she called you, right?"

Maria tightened her pouty mouth and skeptically nodded, "Uhm-hmmm."

"That thing back there is phenomenal."

"See!" She flirtatiously shoved him as the table erupted. "J'aaalllll! That ain't fuuuuuunyyyy."

Casper was melted by the way she pushed out her bottom lip like a spoiled child. "C'mon, let's see whass'up wit' dat Hot Shot game?"

As Maria led the way over to the basketball shooting game she knew she would easily out-shoot Casper on, she could not say that she didn't like the way he watched her bottom.. When she swiftly looked back, her wavy ponytail swung to gently tap her shoulder, "I wanna see what jour shot look like."

He bit at the side of his lower lip before replying, "What I get if I win?"

A teasing glint appeared in her eyes. "Any'ting chu want." She looked to see where she was going, then quickly added, "Cause jhu ain't gon' win."

Following a match that saw Maria effortlessly run up the score on Casper as she swished shot after shot, she went into the bathroom where she overheard three girls talking about Casper and Bear:

"I'm tellin' you, gurrllll! Them two niggaz is *getting' it!*"

"Uhmm-hmmm!" Another, even prettier girl added. "I wish my man was seein' the type of bag they touchin'"

The third girl smoothed down the Nanette Lepore Latin quarter leather skirt that she wore over black leotards, "Who you tellin'." The lovely light-skinned girl with the honey-colored eyes smacked her lips dramatically, dipped her back and then ghetto-fabulously swirled her shapely rear from left to right. "I'mma walk right up on that nigga Casper, let him see what I'm workin' wit'." She snaked her neck, "And introduce myself. Cause I don't-give-a-fuck!" The two girls with her burst into animated laughter. "Shit! He can put a baby in my belly, tonight!"

"Awl bitch, you just talkin' shit." Her homegirl said as she began to put her things back into her Hermes bag.

Maria continued to wash her hands while the girls went on talking. *Hmmmm,* is what she thought; because it was as if the girls hadn't even acknowledged that she was the one who had been hanging out with Casper all night.

* * *

Casper waited for Maria over by the Skee-Ball game; and when she spotted him—he was mindful of the pigeon-toed, bowlegged steps she took toward him in what had to be the tiniest pair of Air Max sneakers he'd ever seen. "You won a lotta' tickets, huh?" He asked, displaying his overly cocky, crooked grin.

Maria raised her head from her count as she neared him, just as the three girls came out of the bathroom. "I did al'ight." She affectionately brushed her hip against his thigh as she passed, leaving the three glammed-up beauties to gawk in her wake as she led Casper back to their table.

Yeah. Casper knew she knew he was taking a long glimpse, because she put a little something extra into the sway of her super bubbly behind.

Even in loosely fitting jeans, Maria's ass was amazing. She had one of those booties that jutted out, high and tight from her lower back, like a shelf for a guy to sit a bottle of beer on—its two plump cheeks resembling smooth globes that were so firm, yet as pliable as a fresh sponge cake to the touch.

"Sooo," Maria slowed her pace and looked over her shoulder as Casper got close enough to smell the pineapple scent of her shampoo. "are chu coming to our hoop game on Friday, or what?"

When Casper did not answer fast enough, she stopped and caused him to bump into her from behind.

"Oh, my bad." He allowed his hands to encompass her narrow waist, as his chin grazed the top of her silky head of hair. "So, uhh, who y'all playin'?"

"Boy, it don't matter!" She exclaimed while lightly bumping her buns into him in the midst of pulling away. "Is chu comin' or not?" She asked, while walking backwards.

"I'mma come."

During the ride out to Wexford, Casper and Maria sat in the back talking the entire ride—neither one of them could get enough of what the other had to say; and before either of them knew it, Bear was pulling the Hummer to a stop at the bottom of Maria's lengthy driveway.

"Want him to drive you up?" Cidny asked.

"Nada, I don't need mi raise (parents) questioning me about de' different rides pullin' up in de' driveway."

"Right." Cidny released an uneasy little cackle, as she looked back into the back seat at Casper watching Maria pull on her jacket. *Is this fool going to ask to walk her to the door. Or am I gon have...*

Casper finally seized the moment, "Uh, it's dark out. Let me walk you up to your house?"

She softly bit at the inside of her cheek. "It's lit de' whole way up."

"Oh, my gaaaawd!" Cidny humphed and rolled her eyes from the front seat.

Casper gave a languid shrug in response.

"Venga. C'mon." Maria opened the door and stepped down from the truck.

The two began the walk up the tree-lined, winding brick driveway—with their jackets unzipped and their hands inside of their pockets.

Casper knew that he didn't have a lot of time, so he bit the bullet and spoke first. "I just want let'chu know that I had a nice time."

"Thank chuuuu." She looked away to hid her giddy grin.

"I like that way you talk, too. That jhu and chu." He tried to imitate the way she pronounced the words.

Maria coyishly nudged him with her shoulder, "Jhu are soooo crazy."

He licked his lips and grabbed a hold of her sleeve, "I'm serious. I love your accent and dat hoarse, scratchy rasp to your voice."

She turned with him still holding on to her sleeve and effectively backed up until they were standing behind the last tree at the top of the driveway—which shielded them from any prying eyes within the house.. "Mi Mother always says that mi voice sounds like this, cause of a youth soccer accident that knocked mi hormones outta whack."

Casper's brow came together as he thought about it. "Oh, like when a boy's voice changes when he's going through puberty?"

"Some t'ing like that. But, it's a long story."

"Oh." He uttered before an uneasy hush came over them.

Maria was quite nervous, standing there in the prolonged silence—her stomach doing flip-flops in anticipation of what might, or might not happen.

Casper gave a slight tug on her jacket sleeve and she looked up from the tips of her sneakers, nearly meeting his eye with her standing higher up on the slope. "Can I kiss you?"

She had been so ready for this, but all of a sudden she'd forgotten what it was that she was supposed to say and do. "I don't know, can you?" Maria hadn't taken a breath in what felt like hours. *Did I just say that? Why did I say that? Uh! That was soo dumb.*

He leaned forward and planted a long, romantic kiss on Maria's soft lips. The first kiss worked so well, that Maria's body seemed to melt into Casper's, until she abruptly pulled back, took a deep breath; then, glared as her nostrils flared while she cracked her chewing gum. CRA-AAACK! CAR-RAAACK!

I thought that went well; But, apparently not. Casper's brain began to bemoan while Maria stood there giving him what he thought was that evil attitude.

Maria turned her head, took the gum out of her mouth and tossed it into the patch of mulch beneath the huge evergreen tree. Next, she took a step and a half to close the space between her and Casper so she could drape her arms over his shoulders.

This time the kiss was an intense French kiss. Hot. His tongue entered her mouth bold and strong—and with her height nearly reaching his with her standing on the up slope, she could feel his hard manhood pressing into her groin. "Hmmmm." She moaned inside his mouth as she shifted her hips slightly. She sensuously sucked his tongue and swirled hers with his, savoring his strength. Maria could not help but groan in the heat and the blissfulness of grinding her awakened loins against his.

Casper's hands were all over her juicy butt, caressing and squeezing the marshmallow-like flesh. It was almost as if his fingers could sink into the softness of her buns. Then he got bolder and slid his right hand up along her rib cage to palm her smooth, heavy breast—mashing the mound and thumbing the hard nipple until Maria's lovely body moved against his with even more of an urgent response.

"Huhhh-mmmm." Maria gasped as a sharp tingle shot from her sensitized teta, straight down to the pebbly button between her panty-less thighs.

She got scared and pulled away. "Boy," She whispered. "jhu betta' watch it with that hand."

"Or what?" He panted in her face and reached back inside her open jacket to grab her at the waist. "I asked to kiss you and I did."

Casper's jaw clenched with anxiousness. Though the word he used was kiss, the look in his eyes read, *I am going to fuck you!*

Maria was frightened for just that brief second or two. But then that flood of warmth swept through her, filling her with confidence. She shifted her weight from one foot to the next, wondering what she needed to do to get him to do what she'd just stopped him from doing—without making herself look like a total slut.

"I wanna kiss you one more time, before I leave." Casper said, confidently pulling her lush body to him.

He leaned in and began to kiss her again, sucking her tongue—savoring the heat and sweetness which she eagerly poured forth from her mouth into his, as he aggressively fondled that same inflamed boob.

"Ummm-mmm!" When he grabbed a hold of her by the ass to grind and swivel his pelvis with hers, Maria had a new rush of delectable sensations. She'd been finger-popping herself for as long as she could remember, so she knew what it was like to experience an orgasm. But with his strong hand mauling her tender teta while the other one roughly pawed her ass, she became swept up in a haze of lustfulness that reached heights she'd never known.

Instinctively, Maria began to hump her sex up and down the length of the bulge his rigid shaft made in his jeans. She was wallowing from the heat and power radiating from his organ; when suddenly her legs began to uncontrollably stiffen, from the top of her thighs to the bottom of her curling toes. "Khu-uhh!" There was no restraint of the sensation that overcame her dewy slit.

Casper felt Maria shudder, just before a hoarse keening sound escaped her throat to vibrate onto his lips. *I know this girl ain't just bust-off?*

Maria tucked her face inside of his coat and moaned softly into his chest. The sensation she felt was a hundred times more wonderful than anything she'd ever encountered. Then she did something that surprised Casper.

She firmly placed her tiny hands against the wall of his chest and pushed away as she slowly backed the rest of the way up the cobblestone driveway with her thighs pressed tightly together. "I gotta go."

Casper stood there for a moment after she disappeared from his sight. *Man! That girl is somethin' special.* He pulled at his saggy jeans and strolled back down the driveway.

Meanwhile, Maria was floating on a cloud as she entered her home and drifted upstairs to her bedroom. She had been practicing how to French kiss a guy with Cidny and a few other girlfriends, since middle school—and none of that prepared her for what just happened. *God! His t'ing was so hard and thick.* It gave Maria sort of a thrilling knot within her belly, just thinking about it. She had seen hundreds of penises in the X-rated movies she'd watched over the years, but nothing was like getting up close and personal with the real thing.

* * *

Casper hopped in the back seat and put on his smooth *Poker Face* until they hit the freeway, "Cid, let me get Maria's number."

She turned sideways in her seat to look back at him. "Bear, peep your boy. Now he wanna talk? What was y'all doin' up there for so long?" Her eyes popped wide-open in wait.

He dropped his chin to his chest and sighed. "C'mon man."

"Uh-uhhhh." Cidny whipped out her phone and smiled jovially. "I'll have to call her first."

Casper sat in back of the Hummer, stewing for the next 10 to 15 minutes while Cidny giggled and tee-hee'd to Maria over the phone. And what vexed him even more, was the fact that she spoke mostly in Spanish.

"Bye-bye!" Cidny squealed, prior to rapidly pressing a number of buttons on her phone before playfully laying her grey eyes on Casper. "Whaaaat! Don't look at me like dat." She exclaimed like she was hurt.

He frowned and poked out his lip. "I thought chu was…" Before he could finish his statement, he felt his cell phone vibrating.

A smile from ear-to-ear broke across Casper's grill, the instant he answered the call. He and Maria stayed on the phone the rest of the ride home. Once at the loft, he continued to talk with her until they both fell asleep with cell phones pressed to their ear.

The next morning, Casper noticed that Master had managed to bust his stitches. "Master! I can't believe you did just what I told you not to!" The pit bull simply looked up from his spot, curled up on the carpet and yawned.

Casper had gotten up early to run around and get some money put together before he drove out to the North Hills to meet up with Fly's old drug connect, Mr. Delgado. But now, he had to run Master by the veterinary office, first.

By ten o'clock, Casper was in perpetual motion; he had picked up money from a few guys and dropped money off at the stash house. He and Bear learned from Fly a long time ago, that it was best to keep money, drugs and guns, in different places that could not be traced back to you. As a result, they would pay older people that they had good relationships with, to allow them to put a hidden safe or two in the basement floor.

After dropping off the last bag, Casper decided to roll through his neighborhood in his Monte Carlo SS.. His hood was similar to most of the ghettos throughout the United States; blocks upon blocks of rowhouses and two-story homes that had seen much better days. The low-income housing dwellers dropped the value of the property around them, which caused most inner city neighborhoods to spiral downward into crime and rundown, or abandoned buildings—making it easy for illegal drugs to flourish in such an open urban market.

But, there was something that made Casper's Wilson Works neighborhood a little different, *The Killer Alleys*. While most hoods were ruled by projects that were nearby, his was ruled by those that had control of the dangerous alleys. And then there were the narrow cuts, and/or short walkways that crisscrossed to sometimes intersect blocks and alleys—allowing a person to easily escape law enforcement, or someone looking to do them harm, or vice-versa in the case of someone looking to surprise their potential victim.

"Yo!" Casper barked good-naturedly into his cell.

"Nigga! Don't yo me." Ramsey, a young lady whose beauty and body were enough to make an average guy beg, bellowed back through the line. "I know you seen me on my stoop when you rode past?"

Ramsey was a Wilson Works chick through-and-through. She had heart, fought like a dude, and she was one of Casper's closest homegirls—one whom he trusted with almost anything.

"Girl, quit trippin'. I was prob'ly checkin' my rearview when I rolled by."

"Mmmm-hmmm!" She humphed, "You know damn well, ain't nobody tryin' to bring your lil'ass no move out in this hood."

He humphed right back, "You neva' know."

Ramsey smacked her thick, full lips. "So, when you get back in the city?"

"Who said I ever left?"

"What 'eva." She drawled in disbelief. "So, is you swingin' by or what? I'm tryin' to get my back blown out."

Casper chuckled at her bluntness, "Yo, youz crazy."

"Nahhh." Ramsey declared, "I just keep it a hun'ed."

The two had been fuck-buddies for as long as either of them could remember. And when they chose to secretly hook-up, it was sexual-napalm.

"Who at da' crib?" Casper asked.

"Nobody. And don't take allll day."

Chapter 19

Casper nodded as he bent the corner and pulled onto the block he'd grown up on. "'Sup Fred, Al?" He hollered out to a couple of old timers standing out in front of the bar on the corner.

There were a few boarded up houses on the street, but for the most part the properties looked neat and there weren't drug sales taking place out in the open.

"Whaa crackin', Loc?" The tall, lanky, brown-skinned young man spoke to Casper from his seat on the stoop between the thick chocolate thighs of the girl braiding his hair.

"Six hun'ed (Love), nigga." He replied, as his man Flame turned to the girl doing his long hair and told her to go inside to grab his bookbag from her bedroom closet.

Sheka sucked her teeth and rolled her eyes as she rose to do her man's bidding. "You ain't gon' be tellin' me what to do." She mumbled, while angrily brushing a few hairs from her smooth, dark thighs, before going inside.

I know you ain't out here showing off? Is the look she received from Flame.

Casper just had to poke some fun at his man, "Yo homie. Is you sure you layin' dat pipe right?"

"What nigga?" He pushed his chest out, "I stay havin' her tender ass screamin' shit in foreign languages."

"Yeah right. I'm thinkin' her young-ass got'chu whipped." Casper added dismissively.

Flame simply smirked and glared.

"So, uhh, what's da milk (word) on da' Hood?"

Flame threw up a gang sign to some guys in a passing car and began to speak, "The work we fuckin' wit' is trash. And niggaz hopin' you gon' get it straight. Period!"

He took a deep breath, paused and looked skyward. "I'm s'posed to holla at Fly's old plug (drug connect) later on."

"Yeah, well you need to get on dat cause da' block gotta get fed. Niggaz is out here starvin'. They-"

"I know, I know! Niggaz got big appetites."

Flame shrugged his wide shoulders, "Aye."

There wasn't really too much more for Casper to say. He needed to speak with his actions or he would loose the Hood before he ever really got the chance to have control of it. "I'm on it, man."

Flame left that subject alone and took the bookbag from Sheka. "Here."

Casper appeared to have a questioning thought prior to accepting the bookbag. "I ain't really tryin' to hop in da' Chevy with all dat bread."

159

"I ain't takin' dat back in dere." Sheka expressed with plenty of ghetto sass as she spread her thighs to sit back down behind Flame, to resume braiding his hair. It did not seem to bother her when the frayed bottoms of her cutoff shorts rode up to the very verge of her crotch.

He turned again and looked his young girl in the eye. "I'mma have Sheka run it around to Nay's crib." Flame said to Casper while speaking to the girl with his eyes.

* * *

Ramsey's Bedroom

"Oh helllll nah!" Ramsey shrieked when she came back into her room and caught Casper pulling up his 7 Brand Jeans. "Where da' fuck you think your funny colored, black'ass is goin'?"

"Ram squad. Stop trippin'." He hurried to buckle his belt when she moved forward like she was going to hit him.

"I ain't playin' wit'chuuu." She whined and weakly resisted, while Casper playfully grabbed her from the side.

"C'mon, dis nigga just hit me on da' jack. I gotta drop him his bag. You know how this game go."

"Uhm-hmmmmm!" She humphed with insolence, "If I knew you was gon' bounce like dis, I would've fucked for your first nutt, instead of bobbin' my mu'fuckin' head."

He began to rub her warm, shapely ass through her sheer La Perla panties. "Girlll, you know how I am when I get up in your sticky lil hot pot. I'm tellin' you. We up in da' hotel, all night tonight."

Casper knew damn well that he wouldn't be returning after receiving a text from Maria, to go out to the show to see the new SAW movie. So, he broke Ramsey off the stack (a thousand dollars) in his pocket and told her to go out to the mall to buy some slutty lingerie.

"What kind?" She purred, while swiftly calculation how much she'd spend and how much she would keep.

"Get some of that Victoria Secret shit so I can watch your fine ass walk around da' room, before I rip it off you." As Casper cupped her bouncy butt cheek, he thought, *Maybe I should hit. 'Cause I know Maria ain't givin' up no pussy tonight...Mmmm! And Ram do know how to throw her hips around.*

Finally, Casper made up his mind to comeback for Ramsey after he went out to the movies and allowed Maria to get him all worked up...

"Hey, whass'up, Leem?" Casper said to Ramsey's uncle, as he bumped into him on his way out their front door.

Now, being the old school gangster that he was, Leem gave his condolences in regards to Fly, patted Casper on the back and schemed, *I know that young nigga eatin',* he watched him hit the Chevy's silent alarm. *He lookin' more and more like my next vic, every time I see his young ass."*

* * *

Casper rushed home, showered and threw on a casual pair of Simon Miller slacks with a Kenneth

Cole turtleneck. Then he headed out to Mr. Delgado's palace in the Hills that sat on the priciest of acres without a neighbor in sight. The place already looked like a colorful paradise and the spring hadn't even gotten into full swing yet. There were manicured and artistically shaped flower beds that burst with azaleas, roses, daffodils and several other kinds of flowers that seemed so out of place this early in the season.

He was led down the long hallway of the multi-million dollar Victorian-style mansion by a lithely moving, slimly built, young beauty that had to be Mr. Delgado's daughter. She spoke very little, but as she opened the French double doors that led to what looked like a plush waiting room, she allowed her finger tips to brush over the back of Casper's hand. *Nah, it ain't even worth it.* Casper thought to himself. *Plus, I need a little more meat to play around with.*

Casper's thoughts were all over the place due to the uncertainty of the situation he presently found himself in. He was nervous. He had no idea if Mr. Delgado would accept his offer. Hell, he had no idea if the man would laugh in his face, or have him murdered for wasting his time.

"Greetings my friend." Mr. Delgado emerged from a door Casper hadn't seen and ushered him into his office. He was a slim, yet strongly built man, with bright intelligent eyes, who appeared to be in his mid-sixties.

The office was spacious, more than 1,100 square feet. The walls to Casper's left and right were dominated by Vintage floor-to-ceiling mahogany bookshelves, containing an assortment of biographies, books on history, business and industry.

Mr. Delgado pressed a button behind the massive, handcrafted wooden bureau he'd once purchased from the Sotheby's auction house. "We can talk freely in here."

"Uh, okay." Looming on the wall behind the desk was a large bear head that Casper could not rip his eyes away from.

Mr. Delgado sat down in his handmade high-backed leather chair and glanced back at what had drawn Casper's attention. "Jhu like mi lee'tle friend, huh?" He tried to speak in measured tones, as if to conceal his Spanish accent, but it did not always come off as he intended.

Casper sat in his seat chuckling, as he listened to the witty and surprisingly funny man tell a story about the grizzly bear being dead-set on having him for lunch while he unknowingly sat on a downed tree, fishing in that particular bear's fishing spot.

"By de' way, Reece..." He said, once he'd finished the story, "What's in de' saco? The bag, I mean?"

"Oh, uhhh, the seventy-five thousand I owed to Fly for the work I had left."

He smiled and fingered the edge of his razor-sharp mustache as he eyed Casper over the bureau. "Si (Yeah)," He shrugged nonchalantly, "This is shocking, because I know how it goes; the product one still has on the street becomes a bonus for those that owed on de' back-end."

Hesitantly, Casper nodded in agreement.

Mr. Delgado waved his hand as if to clear the air. "I'm not going to cry over spilled milk, considering the amount of money Fly brought in over our years together."

He saw his opening and went for it. "Mr. Delgado, that's kind of what I wanted to speak with you about."

The older man rose from his seat and gestured toward another set of doors, but Casper acted like he didn't see; instead, he allowed his eyes to sweep the room, one more time, while he deduced his plight. *I know this guy ain't about to try and rock me to sleep.* He thought, while involuntarily reaching for the handgun that he'd left in the car.

"Reece. C'mon, let us walk and talk."

Mr. Delgado draped an arm around Casper's shoulders and escorted him through the double doors out into an impressive courtyard that exploded with a mass of colors, scents and plants that grew everywhere like a wild yet neat collage of green lace. The gentle rays from the early spring's bright sun sprayed the Spanish tiles that covered the walkways and the patio, along with the benches and chairs scattered in a somewhat orderly seating arrangement, throughout the courtyard.

The daughter arrived with a tray of refreshments and left without speaking a word.

"You are a guest here, no?"

Casper nodded and listened as the man went on to explain in a roundabout way that he was a slow-roller, who could afford to take his time to make his profit because he usually purchased his product up front.

"This way, I have no timetable and it allows me de' freedom to deal with only a few men that I know and trust." He paused, "That I trust to a certain extent."

Both men had a short chuckle, due to that last tidbit.

"Mr. Delgado, is there a way that I could start out by paying for my purchases up front, to earn your trust?" He quickly added, then waited while the man took a brief moment to ponder what seemed to be a deep thought.

"Reece, I can let'chu have kilos for de same fifteen-five as jour uncle Fly." He raised a slim index finger. "But only for a three month period."

Casper could not hope to contain his smile as his dark eyes lit up. "Okay, bu..."

He halted him with that same slim finger, "There's another but... If jhu can't handle fifty kilos, I can't do it because it's too much of a risk for such a small profit."

Casper's chin plummeted to his chest. It was just too steep of a jump for him to make without some kind of safety net.

He understood the young man's predicament. "Look. I'd be willing to do half on consignment. Otherwise." He left it at that.

"Thank you, Mr. Delgado." He reached out to shake his hand, "I can work with that."

"Great!" Their hands grasped tightly together, "We can work out the particulars later."

The two got up from their seats and strolled around the egg-shaped pond, as Mr. Delgado revealed to Casper that his uncle had wanted him to make his money and then get out before his twenty-first birthday came around.

"That's a thought." Casper shook his head from side-to-side to that—and slowed his gait as the subject of Fly's murder came up.

"I assure you. Nothing but revenge came to mind when word of Fly's murder reached me. I had professional wet-workers in transit from out of town." Mr. Delgado displayed a devilish grin for the first time. "But chu seemed to have moved a lot faster than I anticipated."

Casper remained noncommittal as the older man eyed him. "People do what they gotta do." He stated without making eye contact...

As Mr. Delgado watched the young man pull off, his usually accurate gut told him that Fly's nephew would soon move into a position of power.

* * *

Casper pulled onto the crowded freeway and began to mull over the meeting. *I can't believe Fly's slick ass was makin' two stacks off me on each joint.* He could still hear Fly telling him, *'I'm givin'em you for what I get'em for.'*

On a more serious note, he started pondering the task of getting his priorities into order. He turned 20 soon and he needed to decide where he was going with his life. *I ain't sellin' rocks to buy a new pair of kicks no more. And I ain't tryin' to become another Ghetto Superstar living out a life behind nobody's prison bars.*

On that long ride home, Casper would put together a plan to sell the new kilos in its uncut powder form, instead of taking the risk to cook it up into crack cocaine—which would ensure the pitchers (drug sellers) a more valuable and potent product when it was mixed with baking soda and whipped into rock.

"Niggaz gon' come-the-fuck-up!" He shouted.

Casper clearly understood that one's time in the drug game did not last forever. Either you will eventually fuck up and get yourself caught or murdered; or some snake-nigga would do it for you by selling you to law enforcement for his own time-cut.

"Let me see, I got almost 200 thousand saved..." He switched lanes. "If I can reach three million cash... I'm done. I'm out!" He stated emphatically.

"Niggaz always think they can ride this drug dealin' shit til the wheels fall off. Nah!" Casper continued to hold a conversation with himself. "Ball until you fall. Ride hard til my number gets called... Uh-uh! Not me, player."

His phone began to vibrate on his hip, "Them sayings all sound good until you get knocked."

He looked down at the phone and read the text from Maria, *I was just thinking about you and what we talked about last night. Can't wait to see you this evening.*

He laughed because Maria had persistently explained to him that what happened at the top of her driveway, was a first.

Casper wasn't all that adapt with the texting craze, but he did what he could, *It ain't about nothing, babe. We just getting started.*

She sent him back a smiley face.

Chapter 20

Two narcotics officers, Johnson and Link, were working the East End section of the city and had the part-time informant, full time crackhead, Bunbenny, hemmed up on one of the Wilson Work's dark side streets.

"What's up, Benny?" Officer Johnson growled while tightening his grip on the ash-colored man's throat.

Even though Officer Johnson's skin was darker than the man who he was currently choking, he was still more of a racist than his white partner.

"C'mon, Tom. I mean, Officer Johnson." Bunbenny quickly corrected himself as the side of his face was smashed against the rough texture of the brick wall. "Hoo-ohhh! Yo, hold up!"

"What'cha got?" Link yelled from over by the grey Caprice Classic sedan—playing the good cop for the day. "Ben," he lazily shrugged his slim shoulders, "you know my partner don't care too much for niggaz."

"Look." His bulging eyeballs went from one crazed cop to the other. "Uhm, I-I'm tryna tell y'all dat Casper's supposed to of come up on a new connect."

It's only been two weeks since Casper flooded the block and already, one of his predictions had taken place… A nigga rattin'!

"What he movin'?" Johnson asked as he slid his leather gloved fist down to grasp Bunbenny by his grimy collar.

"He got coke. Dat primo shit!" His eyes continuously darted here and there like a nervous animal looking to escape. "Dey say it's comin' back on the cook-up, like da' old school powder from the early nineties."

"Whoa!" Johnson's nose wrinkled into a snarl as the stench of the man's fart reached his nostrils. He shook his head, "I didn't ask you all that shit! I said, what'chu know 'bout dat boy murkin' them two Westside Crips that supposedly did his Uncle Fly?"

The crackhead's eyes seemed to gape even wider when a car slowly rolled by. "Re-real talk, Johnson. I heard dat Fly's old connect had some O.T. (out of town) hitters do them boys."

The cop let go of Bunbenny's collar and reached down into the side pouch of his military cargo pants for a plastic bag full of crack-rock. "Here." He sprinkled a few of the tan-colored rocks into the addict's dirty hands. "Take this too."

Bunbenny looked down at the rocks and the officer's card dangling between his fingers. "Oh, okayyyy. I'm, I'mma call soon as I he-hear somethin'." He stammered while he tweaked to go blast the drugs into his worn-out lungs.

169

Johnson yelled out, "Call me!" From inside of the car as the crackhead disappeared into a partially collapsed abandoned building.

Later that same night, Cidny and Bear were seated at a table inside the Aqua, a high-end downtown nightclub that catered to a diverse crowd. Its waterfall and its glass encased walls and floors of flowing white water were a major attraction which would continue to amaze guests, even after their first visit.

"Bear, I gotta pee." Cidny said softly while placing her mai tai next to his tumbler of Hennessy.

He watched as she rose from her seat to tower at nearly 6'8" in her overpriced, ankle-strapped heels. "We out, when you get back."

Arching her back for effect, Cidny adjusted her generously sized knockers inside the cups of the blue, strapless Jason Wu frock that was cut dangerously high up on her healthy sandy-brown colored thighs. "What if I ain't ready to leave?"

Bear leaned way back in his seat and reached between his gaping legs to re-position his package. "Keep it up."

She pushed her fully plumped lilac colored lips out into a pucker before batting her lashes, "You know, when you get it up. I love knocking it back down."

Cidny's eyes seemed to rest on Bear's crotch for a longtime, then she turned on her heels to make her way through the crowd on her way to the ladies room—where things turned from good to bad:

"Uh-uhnnnn! Gurrrlll! That big, horse-faced lookin' bird think she cute." Cidny could hear the girls outside the stall talking about her.

"Fuck-dat-hoe!" Another young woman voiced, "I know she don't think she look betta' than me. Shit! When I used to hook-up wit' Bear, he couldn't get enough of what I had to give him."

Carla, looking strikingly cute as her brown skin glistened with a light sheen of sweat from dancing—added her two cents to boaster her homegirl who used to hook-up with Bear in the not-so-distant past. "Did y'all see her hands!"

"Whoa!" The second girl exclaimed, "Man hands."

"And!" The girl wearing the silk jumpsuit, whose big mouth had started it all—woofed, "I think dat dumb'ass Bitch cut her fuckin' eyes at me, too!"

Cidny came out of the stall with her chin held high and proceeded to leisurely wash her hands while the girls continued to talk about her, but in more of a hushed tone.

"Pshhh! Gurrrl.. I can tell she don't know what to do wit' a nigga like Bear." One of the girls said under her breath; a tad too loud.

Cidny turned and laid her intense grey eyes on the group; consequently, causing the group of young ladies to go deathly silent. "Don't let these six hun'ed dolla Jimmy Choo's dat Bear bought, fool ya. Cause I will take des mu'fuckaz off and whoop all y'allz ass." She clenched her right fist so hard that the knuckles actually cracked.

Cidny had never been in a real fight, yet, the way she'd beat up on that heavy bag whenever she and Maria worked out with Mr. Coleman—she knew she would do some damage.

The girls remained as quiet as a group of church mice, until Cidny gradually swayed her bulbously exaggerated buns out of the bathroom.

"Daaaaamn!" Carla shrilled and began to clown her girls. "She shut y'all hoes da'-fuck-up!"

"Awl Bitch. You ain't say shit, either." The girl wearing the silk jumpsuit replied while painting her lips.

"Let the lil white bitch dat hang wit' her, have been here." Carla assured with an animated nod of her head. She'd heard all about Casper hanging out with his new friend and she did not like it one bit.

"I heard she Puerto Rican." Her girl replied.

"I don't give a fuck!" She sparked, "Mu'tha fuck dat beige Bitch!"

* * *

Instead of getting treated by a horny and very tipsy Cidny, Bear endured the silent treatment for a good twenty minutes before his Boo finally snapped on him inside the Hummer.

"Bear, fuck that!"

"Fuck what? You won't tell me what I did."

Cidny turned to let him see the tears in her eyes. "'Cause you know!"

Bear was trying to drive and find out what was wrong at the same time. "What do I know? Explain it to me."

She tucked in her bottom lip and shook with anger. "I'm tired of allll-your-bitches playin' games with me."

He placed a hand on her thigh, that was rudely shoved away. "You ain't neva' said nuffin' about dat."

"Why do I have to?" She wiped at her eyes and stared at him, "Huh?"

"I mean, look. Bitches see me out wit'chu all da' time. Of course dey gon' hate."

Cidny sniffled, then began to pout like a little girl who just needed to be comforted.

"Listen. I'll do whatever you want me to."

She sat up in her seat. The once docile Cid that he'd met on that chilly evening down on the Oakland campus was long gone. "I want them bitches to stop callin' your phone. I don't wanna hear, *'Oh! She just my homegirl.'* None of dat!"

Bear pulled the truck over and shifted it into park so he could look her in the eye. "I don't know if you know it, but you are the only one I've ever brought to my crib. You stay with me almost every night. Shit! You even be at da' crib when I ain't home." He threw up his hands, "What else can I possibley do to show you that you're my woman?"

Cidny stared at him through her slitted, smoke-grey eyes for a protracted space in time in which her stare transformed from that livid glare, to a look of almost coyish want. She tilted her head to the side and kind of brought her shoulder up to girlishly touch her cheek, "I probably shouldn't have gotten as mad as I did."

He licked at his bottom lip and placed that same huge hand back on her thigh.

"It's just..." She rolled her eyes as a sigh escaped her lips. "These girls were talking about me in the bathroom and I felt soooo dumb. I..."

173

Bear's always cheerful features changed into something that Cidny had never seen. "Who was talkin' about chu?"

"Uhhh." Her eyes got really big as she watched him check the side mirror, make a u-turn, and head back to the club. "You're scaring me. I don't wanna go back there."

"Nah, I just want chu to show me who it was. I ain't even gon' say nuffin' to 'em."

"Bear, pleeeeease." She leaned toward him and grabbed his forearm. "You're really scaring me, baby. Can we just go back to your place?"

Chapter 21

"Ooooooh, Casper! Oooll! Uhhh! Huhhhh!" Maria panted and sobbed out her pleasures as she stood with her feet spaced widely apart, bent over the back of Bear's couch, with her lace chemise flipped up onto her back—while Casper fucked her like a bitch in heat, from behind. "Ohhh, el sintes riquisimo (it feels soooo good)." She began to fervidly bump, then grind her cushiony cakes back into Casper's pumping pelvis in an effort to reap more of the incredible sensations. "Ahhhiiiiieeeee!"

Following a high-pitched purring shriek of content, Maria dropped her forehead down on her crossed forearms and settled into a steady, skin-smacking rocking motion, until her balance faltered and she started tipping to the left. She knew she needed to move her leg to keep from falling, but it was stiff and did not seem to want to act right.

"Huhhh!" Maria awoke with a start that was so sudden that she had to grab the couch to keep from rolling off of it and hitting the floor.. It took a second before she got her bearings and realized she'd fallen asleep on Bear's couch. *Shit!*

She got up, rubbed at her eye and walked into the dining room in a dazed stupor.

Oh! Maria stopped in her tracks.

Bear sat at the dining room table with his back to Maria, as his head lulled side-to-side to the point that it looked like it might roll off his shoulders—while the back of Cidny's head rose and fell in his lap.

Initially, Maria hadn't heard the tell-tale, rhythmic, wet sucking sounds. But once she discerned the nature of the act in progress she cupped a hand over her mouth, turned on her bare feet and nimbly tip-toed back the way she'd come—only to nearly piss herself when she caught a glimpse of Casper pulling up outside the bay window.

"Oh shit!" Maria gasped before rushing into the downstairs bathroom to rinse her mouth and splash some cold water on her face. She then quickly slid her feet in to a pair of Tommy Bahama sandals, jammed a few sticks of chewing gum in her mouth, grabbed up her bookbag, and dashed to the door just as Casper was coming through it.

"Un momento (Hold up)." Maria laid her palm against the center of Casper's chest and backed him up as she shut the door behind her. She swiftly took in the swag that was dripping from his head to toe. The clean Nike Air Jordan's; The baggy dark colored blue jeans that looked to be as stiff as cardboard; and the fitted Yankee cap which just happened to be casually turned around backwards. "Let's go."

176

Casper gave her a kind of confused look. "I thought we all was goin' to the show?"

"We don't need them." She said with a shrug.

"Uh, al'ight." He watched her move toward the truck ahead of him and wave to one of Bear's neighbors tending to his lawn. Maria was so much more different than the young women he'd usually dealt with. Sometimes he'd be out with her and she would manage to still look cute with a hoodie pulled over her head or while wearing a pair of jeans that were just as big as the ones he'd wear. But today, instead of her customary ponytail she wore her hair down and wavy, and the style matched up perfectly with the knitted Dolce & Gabbana poncho she draped over a pair of tight black pencil-leg jeans.

Maria felt Casper's eyes on her and turned, "We've gone to the movies a few times by ourselves, right?"

He simply displayed that cocksure, crooked grin with a slight nod.

Maria's eyes rolled skyward. She and Casper had been on more than a few dates together, which allowed them to easily grow comfortable with each other's personality in such a short amount of time. "Anywaaaayyyy." She cracked her gum a few times before going on, "I'm sure if Cid wants to go to the movies later on, Bear will get her there."

"Yo, who you talkin' too?" Casper backed her up agaist the side of the truck. "What I tell you about dat mouth?"

"Stop Caaaasperrrr." She purred in a soft whisper prior to tightening her pouty little mouth and looking up at the calm blue sky, in an effort to hide the skittishness that came with his body being so close to hers.

He licked his lips and stepped closer. He knew the affect he had over her. "Your legs is lookin' real sexy today."

Maria sunk her top teeth into her bottom lip and dropped her gaze down over her attire. "Si, they are a lee'tle tighter than dee jeans I usually wear."

Casper moved so that his body was flush to hers, "I wouldn't mind seein' you show off your tight lil frame more often."

The goose-bumps that had broken out all over her skin suddenly began to tingle. "Oh, uh, okay."

To Casper, Maria's legs were amazing. They were somewhat a shorter version of what one would call athletic, or dancer's legs. Her thick, sculptured thighs and tightly muscled calves were proportioned perfectly with the rest of her shapely little body. "You got legs like a dancer."

Maria eased around him and got up into the passenger side of the truck while Casper went and got into the driver's side. "I dance." She replied, as he started the truck.

Casper looked at her like, *I know you ain't stripping on the side.*

Maria's pug nose wrinkled. "Nada!" Her green eyes slitted, "Formal dance, Casper. I've trained in classical, ballet and African dance."

"Oh, excuuuuuse me." He twisted and rolled his neck to mock her.

"Nah, uh-uh!" She release that jovial scratchy laugh of hers, "Jhu know chu was tryin' to start some mierda!"

178

"Mier—. What?"

She huffed as she had begun to apply a coat of lipgloss to her lips. "It means shit. Jhu was tryin' to start some shit. I'mma have to teach jhu some Espanol."

"Amongst other things." He mumbled while taking a sneak of a peek at her glistening, amazingly kissable lips.

With a local radio station playing over the truck's stereo, they rode out of Bear's neighborhood in the silence of their own thoughts.

Every time I have a dream about this guy, he ends up bending me over and doing it to me, tipo perra (doggy style)! What is wrong with de' missionary position, Maria? Dios (God)! She pondered while silently staring out of her window at the unseasonably warm spring day.

Meanwhile, Casper was in the middle of pondering his own thoughts. *Man! What do I gotta do to get this girl to let me get between her thighs. Healthy thighs, I might add.* He glanced over at the way she sat in the seat with one leg tucked up under the other. Casper could hear Bear's deep voice in his head right now, *Cuuuzzzzz! You got's to get down dere an lick dat pearl button for her. I'm tellin' you, she'll be beggin' you to bust it open.*

The black Chevy truck pulled to a stop at the red light and without thinking about it, Maria turned her head and gleeked a projectile of spit that cleared the sidewalk to strike the fence post she'd been aiming for. *Dios mios (Oh my God)!* Her raspy voice screamed inside of her head. *I can't believe I just spit out de' window. Did he see me?*

SPLLL-AAAAT!

This wasn't the first time that Casper saw Maria spit; nonetheless, he played it off and acted like he had missed her little mishap by focusing in on the rush hour traffic.

Maria tucked in her chin and slyly checked to see if Casper was paying attention—when she was certain he wasn't, she swiveled in her seat to face him, "Uhhh, Papi. Where are chu taking me?"

Casper could not help but smile. The girl was just too enticing, even when she wasn't trying to be. Thus, he decided to toy with her a bit.

He began to scratch at his neatly trimmed chin hairs, "I mean, look. The movie don't start til like 7:30. So, I was gon' swing by my crib." He looked away to check the side mirror as he switched lanes. "To ahhh, you know. Kill some time."

Maria shook her head vigorously. "Uh-uh! Nada! I...I, I..." She suddenly ceased the stammering, humphed, criss-crossed her arms over her plump breast, then pushed out her bottom lip like a spoiled two year old. "Casper, I told chu. I-am- not-stepping foot in jour casa by mi self."

"Jelly, I'm..."

She pursed her glossy lips and shook her head undauntedly, "Uh-uhhh." Using the index finger on her left hand, she moved a few unruly locks out of her face and pushed them behind her ear. "I don't know what'chu might do to me."

Casper looked directly into her eyes. "I ain't gon' ever do nuffin' to you that you don't want me to."

A gasp of breath rushed from her lungs so fast that she was sure it smacked him in the side of

180

the face. Then she sat there staring, with a dumb look on her face, until the stop light finally changed.

Dios Mios! Maria exhaled a second breath after what felt like two minutes. *His eyes are so deep.*

There was already no doubt in Casper's mind that Maria wasn't the type of young lady he could beguile with a few trinkets of jewelry and a suite inside of a high-end hotel.

I am not sure if the way he looks at me scares me or excites me. Maria mused.

"You know, I was just playin' about swinging by my crib. Right?" Casper spoke as if he just read her mind.

Maria playfully puckered her pouty, pink-colored lips as she scrolled through a text from Cidny on her phone. "Casper, jhu play too fuckin' much." She said while her petite thumbs rapidly tapped the characters...

Cidny had started out questioning her about why she left the house. But when she found out that she'd left with Casper, she began to ask if she was going to give up the goodies.

No! She texted back. *He will not be putting his banana in mi kitty. ATS (anytime soon).*

Y not?

IMnotEZRU (I'm not easy, are you)

ABSO

IIT (Is it tight)? ☺ Maria grinned devilishly.

ABSO...Wellll NRN (Not right now)

HOYEW (Hanging on your every word)

☺ *MWAH* Cidny sent a sweet kiss to her BFF.

NWTDM (Not with that dirty mouth)

SETE (Smiling from ear-to-ear)

181

PTMM (Please tell me more)

Cidny looked up from where she stood in the middle of the living room texting Maria—while naked from the waist down. "Hey, Big Bear." She said in a tiny voice as he came down the stairs, bare chested. *SMH (Shaking my head).*

"Girl, what'chu doin' walkin' around down here wit' no clothes on?" His eyes dropped to her neatly trimmed pubes.

"I'm about to put some on right now." She went around the opposite side of the couch to avoid him.

A huge grin turned up at the corners of Bear's mouth, "What's wrong wit'chu?"

She gave him an odd look with her big, almond-shaped eyes. "Don't play. You know damn well tht you just killed it."

With that said, Cidny headed gingerly up the stairs as her thumbs agilely tapped out a text..

The way Maria continued to blush and roll her eyes as she texted back and forth with Cidny, had not gone unnoticed by Casper. "Damn, what's Cid sayin' to you?"

"Huh!" Maria nearly jumped out of her seat at the sound of his voice. "Oh, nu'ting."

He gave her a knowing, sideways glance. "Yeah, al'ight."

TNT (Till next time). Maria signed off on the message and then flashed Casper a cute smile.

He simply shook his head and smiled while checking a message on his phone. "Aye, can you hand me one of those pre-paids out of the glove box?"

Maria handed him the phone and listened to the clipped conversation. *Why didn't he just use de' phone he already had in his hand?* She thought.

"Yeah, man." Casper sent a hasty eye Maria's way as he spoke. "I'mma have to get wit'chu on da' bag tomorrow. I know my dude." He flashed another sideways look while he listened to one of his best clients put in a bid to get the cocaine for his crack house, as soon as possible. "I know, yo… I'mma look out, doe."

Maria twisted her mouth and watched the sights of the freeway fly by her window..

"Go ahead. Spill it." Casper told her after only a few minutes of silence.

Immediately looking back over her shoulder, Maria let it fly, "Do chu t'ink a time will come when jhu won't need to do this?

"Do what?"

Her bottom lip turned up into a frown. "Slang perico, Casper. Sell de cocaine."

He released a long drawn out sigh. "Maria, look. Where I come from, the kids don't grow up thinkin' about goin' to college." His jaw tightened, "Rightly or wrongly, kids out my way grow up wantin' to live like Nino Brown."

Maria nodded in begrudged agreement and went back to watching the traffic from her window as she began to hum the lyrics to the new Alicia Keys song playing over the radio.

"Aye. You feel like checkin' to see what time the movie starts, out at the Wexford theatre?"

Casper took a deep breath, "Yeahhh, that way I can enjoy you without having to watch my back the whole time."

"I knowww." She crooned, "Jhu do seem much more comfortable when we go out to places, outside of de' city."

Maria stopped talking and allowed her gaze to slowly take in all of Casper. The neatly shadowed beard. The dark, almost burnt orange color of his skin. The tattoos covering the visible skin from his wrists, up his arms. Then without actually thinking about it, her bright emerald eyes dropped into his lap. *Hmmmm.*

"What'chu over dere smilin' about?"

She quickly looked away as her cheeks and ears blazed beet-red. "Nu'ting."

"Yo." He laid a hand on her knee. "I think this is the first time I saw you with lipstick on."

Maria blushed again and shyly avoided his dark brown eyes. "It's lipgloss." She mumbled, while digging through her bookbag. "Aqui, here."

She handed Casper a little package with a laced bow tied at the top. And he could not hide his smile as he opened it and pulled out a "New Wave" sports bracelet.

"Papi, it has especial metal woven into de' fabric that's supposed to put all of jour body's mechanics into sync." Maria broke out in an amazing smile before tucking in her bottom lip.

"What?" He was beginning to be able to pick up on all of her sneaky little idiosyncrasies. "Say it."

"Maybe it will help with jour jump shot." "Oh! You got jokes?"

The two of them laughed and then Maria directed Casper to a quiet little park near her old high school, where they could kill some time until the movie started…

"C'mere!" Casper stepped over into the grass to grab her from behind when she tried to get away from him. "I asked you... When-is-you..." He growled as his wiry arms cinched tightly around her stomach, effectively pulling her back against his hard body. "...gon' come over and cook for me?"

"Haa! Ahaaa!" Amid bouts of fluttery laughter, Maria tugged at the ungiving forearms holding her captive. "I—I! I said I woooould... one dayyy!" She continued to wiggle and squirm her soft assets, counter to his body in an attempt to get free.

IN struggling, all Maria truly succeeded in was the enhancement of Casper's libido with the way her boobs pressed into his arms while her rump smashed flush to his groin. She was far from slow, though. Maria knew exactly why Casper wanted to get her alone at his place. They had gone on enough dates the past few weeks for her to discover just how bad he wanted her cookies.

"Ooooooh!" She promptly stopped squirming, "What is that?"

Even through the denim material of her tight jeans, Maria felt Casper's erection rub brazenly against her bum-bum.

"You know what it is." Casper groaned strongly behind her right ear.

As of yet, Maria had not admitted Casper past second base; however, the thought both frightened and excited her.. "Hmmm." When he widened his stance and bent his knees, she did not stop him from groping for her rapidly swelling globes as his bulge began to move more assertively against her butt.

Casper loved the way he made her body shudder the instant he took hold of a juicy, pillowy

185

melon with each hand. Meanwhile, Maria couldn't help wondering what his penis looked like out in the open.

She imagined a long, thick shaft sticking out over a set of impressive balls, full of creamy man-milk. *No!* Maria's voice screamed inside of her head. She vilified herself—tried to get the picture out of her head. But, she only succeeded in sharpening the vision. "Espera." She gasped, "Wait! I want show jhu sum'ting."

He allowed her to take his hand and lead him deeper into the meticulously kept park. Hand-in- hand, Casper and Maria ventured past precisely goomed trees and bushes, the greenest blades of grass, clipped at what looked to be an exact height. Casper could not remember being in a park so clean. And to make the day even more perfect, there was not a cloud in the soft, baby blue sky.

As Maria guided him over to the white gazebo that sat up on a mound beneath a flowering cherry tree, she looked down happily at her tiny hand clasped within his and noticed the overpowering color of the red fabric woven throughout the New wave bracelet. "Oh! I didn't even t'ink about de' color."

Casper followed her eyes to his wrist. "Girl, you trippin'. I can wear red if I want. I told chu. I ain't all into that, no more."

"Ta'bien (Okay)." She said in a soft scratchy purr.

"See, now dere you go wit' da' Spanish."

Maria licked her lips as she peered up into his eyes. "I got'chu. I'mma give jhu a few lessons."

Though she was born and raised far from Puerto Rico, it was in her; it rippled from the tip of her tongue when she spoke, and it rolled within her curvy hips whenever she moved—Maria could never disguise the abundance of gifts her mother had bestowed on her, no matter how hard she used to try.

"Why are chu looking at me like dat?" She nearly whimpered as she backed up onto the gazebo's mound, bringing her close to his eye level.

Casper sucked smoothly at his top lip, "I still can't get over seein' you with your lipgloss poppin'."

Maria smacked her lips exaggeratedly and sexily shifted her weight to one foot as a hand went to her hip. "There's a lot of t'ings jhu haven't seen from me, yet."

The brow over one eye cocked questioningly, "What'chu mean by dat?"

"Nu'ting." Her eyes drifted downward in an attempt to avoid his, "I don't know why I said that."

Casper embraced her anew, slid his hands underneath her poncho, and began to caress her lower back through the material of her snug t-shirt before bringing his hands down to rest atop of the shelf-like swell of the two, buoyant cheeks. "Girlll, this wagon you carryin' back here is special!"

"Uhh!" Maria twisted her mouth and rolled her eyes skyward.

"I know. I know, dere I go."

"Yuuuup!" She stared unblinkingly into his eyes, as his fingers manipulated the robust, yet softly yielding flesh.

Maria hadn't really decided if she actually had a problem with Casper's adulation for the size and shape of her posterior. To her, it was culturally telling in regards to the praise guys from the inner city heaped on a woman's sizeable butt, as opposed to the opinions most of the guys had where she came from.

"You said you do a lot of squats, right?"

Narrowing her eyes, she cracked her gum in his face. "Jhu gon' find out when we go to de' gym tomorrow."

"So what's up?" His chin jutted forward. "We gon' still hit da' gym at my crib?"

Maintaining the eye contact, Maria silently shook her head from side to side—letting him know, *Ain't nu'ting happening.*

In response, Casper nodded confidently. "You are gon' be mine."

Maria tried to put up a bold front under the heat of his powerful gaze, "Pshhhh! I'm sure that's what'chu tell all de chicas to get what'chu want."

His bottom lip turned up in an arrogant scowl, "Nah, not really."

Stomach fluttering and coiling into knots, Maria stood there on that slope for a long time eyeballing Casper, and the more she looked the more intrigued she became about certain feelings he provoked. *Why him?* She pondered. He was 19, 20, no more than that—dark skinned with a lean, but very stoutly built body. "Mmmmm." Her nostrils inhaled his masculine scent as his hands brushed up and down over the rounded upthrust of her buns.

Following the soft sigh that came in a futile effort to hide the tiny moan she'd just issued, she tried to remember the first time she touched his washboard abs or molded her palms to his chiseled chest, *First date? Second?* It escaped her.

In a demanding tone, Casper uttered, "Get rid of that gum." Which caused Maria to pause as if in a serious debate, before daintily reaching inside her mouth to pluck the gum over his shoulder...

Their lips brushed lightly at first, and then Maria's lips parted and Casper slipped his tongue inside her mouth to lash and entwine with her hot slippery tongue. She titled her head to the side and made a small kitten-like purring sound as her feathery lashes fluttered against his cheek.

When Maria encircled Casper's midsection with her arms and drew him tightly to her body, he began moving his tongue in and out of her mouth in an unmistakable simulation.

Under the assault of Casper's thick tongue, Maria became even more alive. She allowed her own tongue to sweep and thrash his just as aggressively—while rolling her head side-to-side amidst the murmuring moans she sobbed into his mouth. "Hee'eeee." The whimpering moan came stronger this time. She could feel the bulge in his jeans pressing against her itchy sex like a heated pipe, and in a show of unabashed need, Maria squirmed onto it; molding herself to the outlined contours of the organ.

Casper did not miss the sounds she made, nor did he miss the way she arched her back to press her breast forcibly into his molesting hands. "I want'chu." He groaned against her lips while one hand dropped away from a fondled melon to grip a juicy ass cheek, as the other commenced to fumble with her bra until the clasp snapped open.

"Nuh-uhhh!" Maria gasped and half-turned within his arms. Her expression became almost comical as she looked back at him over her shoulder; mouth halfway open in a mix of surprise and opposition.

Instead of giving her a chance to really think about it, Casper suavely gathered up the front of her knitted poncho and her t-shirt. And when she remained silent, motionless, he eased a hot hand up along the smooth skin of her torso to caress and stroke her swollen boob. "Man, I knew you was soft. But…" The sound he made next was one of utter pleasure, which happened to please Maria more than he could have known.

A long sigh escaped Maria's lips as his fingers roughly fondled and squeezed her bare flesh for the first time. "Chu really t'ink I'm soft."

"What!" He replied in disbelief.

Casper went back to kissing Maria's sweet little mouth and in no time he maneuvered behind her to cup and weigh-up her pink tipped mounds with such aptitude that she would have screamed if she wasn't twisting her head back to suck at his tongue like it was his dick.

"Uhmm-hmmmm." He hummed as his mouth closed down over hers. Her mouth was something; made for kissing, made to bring a man straight to his knees while giving more pleasure than he ever dreamed possible.

"Mmmm-huhhhh!" She shuddered back into his mouth as her fires blazed like never before. Then a sudden quiver shook her as she imagined him sucking at her tetas, those masculine lips tugging at her stiff nipples.

While pawing one pulpy breast, Casper's other hand crept down to unsnap her jeans. "Uh-uh!" He husked against her mouth when it appeared that she might jerk away from him. He pressed the palm of the offending hand onto the soft warmth of her shivering belly and let it rest there.

For a moment Casper thought he'd gone too far with her, but when she continued to kiss him he slid his fingers past her tiny, innie-bellybutton; down into her jeans with thoughts of rubbing her kitty through her panties. *Yo! Where's her panties?* At the same time that thought was exploding inside of his head, he pressed his bulge into the crease between her buns and moved his hips from side-to-side to make her feel how hard he was.

Maria mewled a little tune of passion onto his lips that was meant to tell him how much she liked the way he was touching her, "Mmmm. Muh- huhhh." She then leaned back into him as she reached behind her back to grope blindly with one hand until she found it—her flattened palm slid timidly along the bulge his penis made in his jeans.

"Oooohhh!" The gasp burst forth from her as if she'd just realized what it was that she was doing.. A feeling of fear mixed with excitement washed over her once she found his manhood sturdy, and as hard as a tube of marble encased by soft meat.

Casper coaxed her the moment he felt her falter. "Kiss me back." He applied himself with all the skill he had. Reaching down and around the swell of her right hip, his talented fingers glid through her neatly trimmed silk to locate the bud of her clitoris.

"Hoo-oolll! Siiiii, yeh-hessss." Maria hissed in approval as he stroked the pebbly nub. "Uhhhh! Oooooh!" She worked her curved, springy globes back against his pelvis in a hip swiveling motion that hinted of things to come—filling his mind with a lustful haze that threatened to send his throbbing penis bursting through his pants.

In the case of Maria, Casper could actually see himself breaking down to lick and suck at her girl parts until her sweet juices were drained.

Maria hadn't allowed her hand to stay on Casper's vibrant tool for long. But when the strangled, clipped shrill slipped from her throat, she clamped that hand over the hand he had jammed down her pants and continued to issue the tiniest of delightful whimpers as his fingers worked over her oily little pebble.

"Don't be scared. Just let me take you dere." Casper's wet lips had moved to the back of her earlobe, then to the side of her neck—while welcoming her assistance to help drag his fingers up and down and around her tiny button as she worked her hips in a tight circular rotation.

Her nostrils flared and she began grinding back harder, each fervent movement of her pelvis stronger and more insistent then the one before. Then, subconsciously, Casper's fingers dug so painfully into Maria's elastically pulpy left breast that her clitty seemed to pulse and throb beneath his fingers.

"Let it go for me. I wanna hear you." He husked, causing a itty-bitty grunt to slither through her clinched teeth.

Maria bit down on her bottom lip to the point of drawing blood, "Muhhh-uhhh!" She kept her petite hand pressed down atop Casper's in an attempt to increase the pressure on her teta, as the sensations from his manipulation of her pearl nub forced her to bend forward.

Casper leaned over her back with her, "Yeah, dats it." He coaxed.

She sobbed out like a wild animal—the breast that he wasn't mauling swinging freely beneath her layered clothing while his unforgiving fingers repeatedly forced her to spurt like fresh spring water...

"Gaaaawd!" Maria gushed after she managed to wriggle free.

Green eyes wide-open, she backed the rest of the way up onto the sheltered pavilion with her elbows pinned to her body to keep her dangling bra from slipping from beneath her clothing.

Casper's chest heaved with each breath as he came towards her. "Here, let me help-"

"No!" She shook her head and released a shaky giggle, "Jhu are soo-sooo bad!"

"What?" He showed an expression of palms up.

Maria blew a puff of air to get a few unruly locks of wavy hair out of her face. "Boy." She screeched. "I cannot believe jhu just did me like that."

Casper came closer, his chin rising confidently as his dark eyes slowly took in all of her flushed beauty. "I told chu. I ain't gon' ever do nuffin' to you that you don't want me to."

Eyeing him almost skittishly, she finally got her bra's clasp to catch. "Casper, I'm not giving jhu mi cookie"

A very cocksure, crooked grin broke across Casper's grill as he nodded assuredly. "I'mma get'chu. And the cookie."

"Oh, no jour…" She rolled her neck in protest just before she was snatched up in a bearhug, that had her shrieking and squealing like a ticklish toddler.

Chapter 22

A week and a half later

A very excited Maria stood in front of her floor length mirror getting ready for a double date with Bear and Cidny, along with her man, Casper.

"O! Jhu look really cute." Ms. Toni beamed, as she entered her daughter's bedroom after having spent the better part of the day arguing with her husband over the fact that their child was now a college-aged young woman.

"Mommeeee." She turned and pushed out her bottom lip. "How did it go?"

Toni ran her hand through her hair and sighed. "Jhu know jhu are his nina (baby)."

"Yo se (I know)."

She tucked in her lush lips in a moment of thought.. "It's going to take some time."

Sadly, Maria looked down at the floor until her mother reached out to gently to touch her cheek. "Que (Huh)?" She looked up, near tears.

"I'm so glad to see chu dressin' like a young lady." Toni stepped back as she gracefully used a hand to direct her child's gaze, up and down her voluptuous figure. "I no pass jhu all de' body for nu'ting."

"Ma!" She blushed like a little girl and looked away.

"Shit! Act like chu don't know." The proud mother was sick and tired of people thinking she had two sons; instead of the bellos hija (beautiful daughter) with the brains to match, that stood before her.

"C'mon Mom. Dere chu go tryin' to be down."

"I am down. And speaking of being down." A hand went to her hip. "Y tu (How about you)?"

"Como decir (What do you mean)?"

"Are chu using protection?"

The question caught Maria off guard. "Uhhh." It took a second for her to ponder how to work her reply.. "I'm not having sex, yet."

Toni exhaled slowly and nodded accordingly. "Ta'bien (Okay), but…" She eyed her daughter only the way a mother could. "I see how jhu have come outta jour shell. And I know Cidny's doin' it. Sexo, I mean."

That last little tidbit almost knocked Maria off course. But no, she managed to maintain her composure. "So, I'm not."

Toni shrugged, "I'm just sayin'."

Maria's nostrils flared and her pug nose wrinkled into a cute snarl. "Ma! Jours not even listening to me."

"Mieda (Hey)! Who chu t'ink chu talk to?" She ended her daughter's rant immediately. "I hear what'chu say but'chu no hear."

"Que?" Maria changed her tune and questioned meekly.

"Jhu say, yet. No?"

"Si, Ma. But, it's only a figure of speech."

She threw her head back and laughed that high-pitched laugh of hers. "Un buen chiste (That's a good one)!"

Maria began to pout again, until her mother leaned in and spoke in a hushed tone.

"Mi know chu nada bien (not good) with de' pill. So, I'mma see about a diaphragm."

Her brow raised and her breath caught in her chest. The only thing Maria's brain could comprehend was Casper. Their relationship had progressed past kissing and grinding, to some very intimate fondling. In fact, she'd become quite adapt with her hot little hands. But she knew that wouldn't keep a guy like Casper sated for long—and therein lie her problem.. Sometimes she was afraid to even picture his penis, painfully squeezing inside of her panochita (little vagina), yet then, there were other times when that was all she could think about. *Then what?* She would always ponder. Where would she be after the thrill of the chase was over? Would Casper simply move right on to the next challenge? Or, could she use her feminine wiles to hold his undivided attention the way her mother had with her father.

"Maria!"

"Que, huh?" She snapped out of the daydream.

197

Ms. Toni stood there with her hand on her heavenly hips, and shook her head. "De boy that picks jhu up and drops jhu off at de' bottom of de' driveway. He on jour cerebro (brain), huh?"

Maria held up a hand to show her thumb and index finger a few inches apart. "Just a lee'tle bit." She said with a smile as her mother turned up her tiny pug nose in a display of feigned haughtiness.

"Well." Toni offered with a cute smirk. "If jhu any'ting like jour Mama, he gon' need a lot more than that."

"Uh! Mom'meeee!"

She had a good laugh due in part to Maria's embarrassment.. Up until a few weeks ago when Toni spied Maria outside the front door in a heated lip-lock with a young man, she'd worried that her daughter was uninterested in the opposite sex. And being the type of woman that cherished her wifely duties like they were ingrained into her DNA—she could not wait to give her child a few pointers on how to keep a smile on her husband's face. *Oh! Am I being too atrevida (presumptuous)?* She gushed inwardly, as she assisted Maria with the proper coordination of her outfit.

As Toni held up another blouse for Maria to try on, she anxiously chewed at the inside of her bottom lip before broaching a question. "So, uh, Jeally. When am I going to meet dis friend of joursss? De' one that has jhu walking around de' house wiff' dis huge smile on jour cara (face)."

Maria huffed and puffed, to buy time... "Pshhh! Ma, chu already know how Dad'dddy is."

She pursed; then twisted her mouth while she watched her undo the first few buttons of the partially sheer top. "Maria!" Toni suddenly screeched.

In a move that came way too late, Maria turned and pulled the blouse closed to cover the pink hickie that rose over the inside swell of her cream-colored left teta. "It's a rash, Ma!"

Her head shook side-to-side prior to her screeching, "Lee-meeee seeee!" with all the excitement of a flighty high school girl.

"Ma, don't tell he'eeeem. Por favor (please)." Maria whined, causing her mother to look up from inspecting her breast with a look that said, *Now why in de' hell would I do some dumb shit like that.*

Chapter 23

<u>Two Days Later</u>

Casper and Bear sat inside of a nondescript Buick sedan parked on the lot of a Taco Bell that was located a block or so away from the notorious Eastside Garden Town housing project, a housing development so large that two Trackstone projects would fit inside of its limits with room to spare. But unlike the Trackstone projects, this project was ruled by the GTP Bloods.

"Yo man." Bear spoke as he continuously watched their surroundings, "I hope your Blood homie don't got us sittin' here waitin' to get our tops popped."

Casper looked at him, smirked, then looked away.

They were waiting to meet up with Lefty, a GTP Blood, who just happened to be one of Casper's boys since their middle school days. Now Bear, he wasn't as excepting of the GTP's . He always felt that they were responsible for the bullet that shattered part of his knee cap.

"Aye." Bear tapped Casper's knee. "I know you fucked dat niggaz sister back in da' day."

Casper shook his head and went on ignoring him, even though the accusation had struck up a few thoughts of Lefty's sister, Flower. He started reminiscing about her slim, yet curvy little body and those hypnotizing light-brown eyes.

Flower had always been a cute girl to Casper, even with the tiny freckle-like spots she had all over her face, from picking at her chicken pox. And his feelings only got stronger after the night he'd passed by her open bedroom door on his way to use their bathroom.. He could picture her as clear as the day, standing in front of that shade-less lamp that sat on the floor beside her bed—giving him an amazing view of each and every lovely curve beneath the Hello Kitty nightgown she wore that night.

"He pullin' in da' lot." Bear said in a voice filled with irritation.

Casper quickly shook off the haze from his thoughts, got out of their car and got into Lefty's.

"What's up, Blood?" Left barked cheerfully while holding out his fist, for the pound that eventually came.

"You got jokes, huh?" Casper grinned just as playfully. "Y'all niggaz don't wanna see me banged-out, again."

Lefty, a handsome light-skinned young man with the same light-colored eyes as his sister, casually waved Casper off. "Whatever, nigga."

"Yeah, al'ight." His chin jutted up and out, confidently.

"Anyway doe." Lefty said with a slight chuckle, "Yo! That powder comin' back real brazy!" He excitedly bragged on the potent cocaine that Casper was pitchin'.

He slid a dark bag containing the other half of the money, over to Casper.

"You want two more?"

Lefty adjusted the bill of his red, Chicago Bulls fitted cap. "Nah, foe mo'." He wanted double than what he'd started out with.

Casper's brow arched in mild surprise. "Yeahhh."

"Fuck it, man. I'm farmin' this shit out."

He shrugged, "You already know how we roll. Do you, homie."

"Right."

Casper went on to ask if Lefty was still having problems with the squad from the up-top section of his projects.

"Uh-uh, nah. Once main-man bit it, them niggaz fell all the way back."

A GTP O.G. had come home from prison with thoughts of taking half of what Lefty built up. But when his body got filled up with bullet holes outside of a state halfway house, those thoughts were laid to rest right along with him.

"Here." Lefty handed Casper a piece of paper. "That's Rock's O.T. spot."

"Who? Rock dat shot Fly?"

"Yuuup! He down dere fuckin' up change for some Piru's from outta Jersey." He sucked his teeth, "Da' fool green-lighted and he don't even know it."

"Good look, man. I'mma make it happen." Casper shook his man's hand and exited the car with the duffel bag hanging down by his feet, out of the sight of prying eyes..

"Yo! Bear, you ain't gon' believe this shit."

Bear was not as accepting of the information as his boy. "Cas, he's not just gon' give up a fellow Blood."

"See, you on some otha' shit. And don't sit dere and try to act like you ain't never spanked (murdered) no Crips before."

Bear glared at him as he turned out of the parking lot. "Lil nigga, you drivin'."

"Fuck dat! We flippin' for dat shit."

"Both ways?" Bear suggested.

He shrugged, "Why not?"

Casper promptly lost the coin toss and was forced to drive all night, until they reached the small West Virginia town early the next morning.. They quickly found Rock's apartment building, and then scouted the immediate area.

Casper had been to the small town a time or two. It was a once prosperous coal mining and steel mill town, that died a slow death a long time ago. But for the young ghetto entrepreneurs that chose to make their way from the urban jungles to the redneck occupied rural town, there were bags of money to be made. And as long as they stuck with the plan, *Hit it hard for 4 or 5 months, then move out before the indictment process got rolling,* they would get a chance to spend the fruits of their labor.

"Cas. Peep da' super thick white girl." Bear spoke out of the side of his mouth as they sat in the Buick, parked up the block from Rock's building, disguised as old men.

"That has to be dat niggaz bitch." Casper could tell by the way the young woman swung her jean-filling hips, that she did not fit with the town.

The healthy white girl they were watching went by the name of Swin. She wore her hair like a black girl, brandished an ass like a black girl, and had all the attitude to go with it.

Swin never saw the young men sitting in the parked car with their old-time woolen plaid hats pulled low, nor did she notice the shoddy way Bear wore the grey costume dust on his facial hair and eyebrows.

Meanwhile, neither Casper nor Bear failed to miss how Swin killed the extra tight Gucci jeans she wore paired with a short, red leather jacket that was cut just right to show off the ass that she was so proud of.

"Hey!" She waved to a group of boys riding skateboards in a nearby lot, as her bright red platform stripper pumps clicked loudly atop the sidewalk and pushed out her booty even more provocatively than it already was.

Swin was born and raised in this particular small town, a town that saw her aspirations grow as her looks and style allowed for her to be whisked away on trips by a number of the drug dealers that passed through the town even as far back as her high school years. Then, while she was up in New Jersey visiting her girl who had lucked up and gotten herself wife'd by a major baller—she met Rock and thought she'd bagged her own major baller. Until she brought him back to her town to get his money right and found out that she bagged nothing more than a lame-ass hustler, who liked to beat her ass for the slightest infraction, real or imagined.

I hope dis nigga ain't on no Gorilla Pimp shit. Swin thought to herself as she put the key into the door, *Bible! Next time he puts hands on me, it's a wrap. That shit was kind of a turn-on at first. Gettin' knocked around a lil bit before he dicked me down.* She slowly turned the key in the lock to make the least amount of noise. *But fuck all dat. That shit is dead now.* A tingle came to her groin at the thought of her young friend she'd spent most of the morning with.

Meantime, in the bedroom an already heated Rock hopped out of the bed at the sound of Swin entering the apartment. First, he was mad that she wasn't there to knock down his morning boner. Then, he got even more pissed when he saw the way she was dressed.

"Bitch!" Rock growled as he strode across the room wearing a big pair of heart covered boxer shorts, with his barreled-chest thrust forward. "What da' fuck did I tell you?"

"Rock." Swin whispered, pushing out both hands in front of her, in an attempt to fend off the blow she knew was sure to come.

WHA-AACCKKK! She took the open hand to the side of the head, and cried out as she went sprawling to the floor.

He gripped himself and sneered from above her. "You out dere lookin' for some otha' dick, huh?"

"Uh-uh, Rock, no." Swin looked up from the floor with the sweetest, pleading puppy dog eyes, before crawling over on her hands and knees. "I would neva' step out on all dis." She hissed as her soft fist began to stroke his stiffening tool, "Uummm." Her tongue flicked out to lash the helmet-shaped head prior to sucking the heavy meat inside her skilled mouth.

The blond-haired young woman proceeded to give Rock a blowjob to remember for the rest of his life.

Chapter 24

Casper and Bear waited a good twenty minutes after the white girl they presumed to be Rock's woman went inside the building. Then they went around the back to see if they could gain entry.

"Hold up." Casper grabbed Bear by the arm and pulled him behind the wall of the garage that sat diagonal to Rocks apartment building.

A dark-colored SUV pulled to a stop beside the building's side door and let out a black teenager who wore his jeans hanging down off of his butt. Shortly after that, two more teens got out of the SUV and were let into the building through the side door that was held open by none other than Swin.

"Cuz, did you see dat shit?" Bear gasped.

"Did I?" Casper saw everything—even the red bandanas that swung from the right pocket of two of the guys.

"I hope ya man's ain't walkin' us into no cake bake."

Casper chose not to honor Bear's comment with a response, "Look man, I'mma go pull the ride closer; in case we gotta get up outta here with the quickness."

"Nah." Bear stopped him before he could leave. "I'll grab it. If it gets funky out here, you got a better chance on foot than my big ass."

"You right." He chuckled. "You do stick out like a sore thumb."

"Nigga, fuck you."

Casper gave him a light shove and pointed toward the adjoining street. "Park over dere. And if we gotta get ghost, take this street all the way down to the intersection, then swing back around to the gas station we picked to meet up at."

* * *

Casper stood beside the wall and watched as the three guys struggled to get a big rolled up rug through the side door and into the back of the SUV, before the driver went over to the white girl—palmed her by the ass, and threw his tongue down her throat. "What da fuck?" He mumbled under his breath.

After the SUV pulled off and the girl went back inside, Casper eased down to look around. He found fresh drops of blood on the ground, which convinced him to try his luck with a trip around to the front of the building..

"Whoa!" Casper jumped out of the way in a show of agility that belied his disguise, as a little white kid nearly ran him down with his skateboard.

"My bad, dude!" The kid said as he opened the same front doors that Casper thought were locked.

Casper entered the building and cautiously made his way up the stairs to the door numbered 17, where he then took another huge gamble. He titled the front of his hat down even lower and knocked…

When Swin heard the two sharp taps at her door, she never thought to check the peephole—thinking it was her young friend returning for a taste of what she'd promised. "Bishop, I told you…" A high-pitched shriek escaped as she stepped back at the sight of the silencer pointing directly at her face.

"Where Rock?" Casper asked as he slid into the apartment and closed the door behind him.

Swin wrapped her arms protectively around herself and took another shaky step backwards, "Whoooo are you?"

In a low tone, he asked again. "Where is Rock?" As the strong smell of bleach and pine cleaner whirled around his face.

"He-he's not heeeeere." She answered in a whiny voice.

Casper noticed the pink handprint that partially covered the left side of her forehead, and the disarray of the living room. "Whass'up?" He slowly lowered the gun to the side of his thigh.

Swin was far from slow; thus, she easily saw through the disguise to put the puzzle together.. She puckered then twisted her lips before allowing a light grin to crease her red painted mouth. "Did you come a long way?"

He turned up his bottom lip and shook his head as he tucked the long end of the silencer equipped handgun in his waist. "Nah, not dat far."

Salaciously, her tongue slipped out to wet her lips. *Uhm, he a dark skin nigga, too.* Her bright eyes searched Casper's face. *Just how I like my men.*

Casper's eyes roamed the room, while Swin pushed back her shoulders and forced her opulent C-cups forward.

"I feel kind of bad that you came all this way to get beat to the punch… so to speak."

"That's how it goes sometime." Casper was not shy about allowing his eyes to rest on her lush knockers.

Swin smiled, craned her neck to the side, and shoved her hands into the back pockets of her skintight cutoffs. "You know, uhh. You could probably do anything to me that you wanted and I wouldn't be able to identify you."

Casper allowed what she just said to sink in for a moment. *Yeahhh, if I wasn't finally getting' up in Maria's fine ass tonight.*

* * *

"Damn! She scandalous." Bear blurted out as Casper started to tell him the story.

"That ain't even the half of it." Casper said as he went on to tell the whole story as he blended the Buick into the high way traffic, set the cruise control, and headed back up North.

"Yo!" Bear's voice boomed inside the car. "She was tryin' to buss' it open for you?"

"Was she?" He rolled his eyes at what could have been. "Cuz, I'm tellin' you. I think getting' dat nigga murdered turned her the-fuck-on!"

"Man! That bitch gutta!"

210

Casper's head shook, supportively from side-to-side. "Nah, she just got tired of dat nigga beating her ass."

"Yeah, you prob'ly right about dat." He nodded in an endorsing manner. "Puttin' your hands on a chick is sucka' shit, anyway."

"He got what his hand called for, literally." Casper said as he watched Bear snuggle into a comfortable position to sleep. "Man you ain't shit!"

Bear looked at him and said, "Coin flip." then pulled his jacket over his head.

Casper mumbled a few curses, popped the top on a bottle of energy drink, then poured the unpleasant contents down his throat. He had hours of driving ahead of himself on virtually no sleep, and he was supposed to take Maria out to the Comedy Club tonight.

COMING SOON!

Casper II	Ganadores Y Perdedores (Winners and Losers)
Casper III	The Same Things That Make U Laugh Can Make U Cry
Casper IV	*Title not yet released*
Casper V	Blurred Lines
Casper VI	*Title not yet released*
Casper VII	*Title not yet released*
Casper VIII	Lady Boss
Casper IX	*Title not yet released*
Casper X	*Title not yet released*

Order Form

Name: _____

Address: _____

_____

City:_____State:_____Zip: _____

Ship To: ☐ **Address Above**   ☐ **Address Below**

➢ *If you would like to send a copy of CASPER to a friend or family member in a Correctional Facility, <u>please include their Inmate I.D. number</u>, to ensure proper and prompt delivery.*

Name: _____

Address: _____

_____

City:_____State:_____Zip: _____

Book Cost:	**$15.00**
<u>**Shipping:**</u>	<u>**$5.99**</u>
Total:	**$20.99**

☐ Enclosed is a check/money order in the amount of $20.99.

➢ *If you are sending a personal check, please allow 3-5 business days for check to clear.*

Mail this form with payment to: **COTORRA BOOKS**
c/o CASPER - Book I
P.O. Box 37118
Oak Park, MI 48237

Also available at cotorrabooks.com

2

Order Form

Name: _____

Address: _____

_____

City:_____State:_____Zip: _____

Ship To: ☐ **Address Above**   ☐ **Address Below**

➢ *If you would like to send a copy of CASPER to a friend or family member in a Correctional Facility,* <u>pleas e inclu de their Inma te I.D. num ber</u>, *to ensure proper and prompt delivery.*

Name: _____

Address: _____

_____

City:_____State:_____Zip: _____

Book Cost:	**$15.00**
<u>**Shipping:**</u>	<u>**$5.99**</u>
Total:	**$20.99**

☐ Enclosed is a check/money order in the amount of $20.99.

➢ *If you are sending a personal check, please allow 3-5 business days for check to clear.*

Mail this form with payment to: **COTORRABOOKS**
c/o CASPER - Book I
P.O. Box 37118
Oak Park, MI 48237

Also available at cotorrabooks.com

Order Form

Name: _____

Address: _____

_____

City:_____State:_____Zip: _____

Ship To: ☐ **Address Above**   ☐ **Address Below**

➤ *If you would like to send a copy of CASPER to a friend or family member in a Correctional Facility,* <u>please include their Inmate I.D. number</u>, *to ensure proper and prompt delivery.*

Name: _____

Address: _____

_____

City:_____State:_____Zip: _____

Book   Cost: $15.00
<u>**Shipping: $5.99**</u>
Total: $20.99

☐ Enclosed is a check/money order in the amount of $20.99.

➤ *If you are sending a personal check, please allow 3-5 business days for check to clear.*

Mail this form with payment to: COTORRABOOKS
c/o CASPER - Book I
P.O. Box 37118
Oak Park, MI 48237

Also available at cotorrabooks.com

Order Form

Name: _____

Address: _____

_____

City:_____State:_____Zip: _____

Ship To: ☐ **Address Above**   ☐ **Address Below**

➢ *If you would like to send a copy of CASPER to a friend or family member in a Correctional Facility,* <u>please include their Inmate I.D. number</u>, *to ensure proper and prompt delivery.*

Name: _____

Address: _____

_____

City:_____State:_____Zip: _____

Book   Cost: $15.00
<u>**Shipping: $5.99**</u>
Total: $20.99

☐ Enclosed is a check/money order in the amount of $20.99.

➢ *If you are sending a personal check, please allow 3-5 business days for check to clear.*

Mail this form with payment to: **COTORRA BOOKS**
c/o CASPER - Book I
P.O. Box 37118
Oak Park, MI 48237

Also available at cotorrabooks.com

Order Form

Name: _____

Address: _____

_____

City:_____State:_____Zip: _____

Ship To: ☐ **Address Above**   ☐ **Address Below**

> ➢ *If you would like to send a copy of CASPER to a friend or family member in a Correctional Facility,* <u>please include their Inmate I.D. number,</u> *to ensure proper and prompt delivery.*

Name: _____

Address: _____

_____

City:_____State:_____Zip: _____

Book   Cost: $15.00
<u>**Shipping: $5.99**</u>
Total: $20.99

☐ Enclosed is a check/money order in the amount of $20.99.

> ➢ *If you are sending a personal check, please allow 3-5 business days for check to clear.*

Mail this form with payment to: **COTORRA BOOKS**
c/o CASPER - Book I
P.O. Box 37118
Oak Park, MI 48237

Also available at cotorrabooks.com

www.ingramcontent.com/pod-product-compliance
Lightning Source LLC
Chambersburg PA
CBHW071334250626
47159CB00004B/1598